Trevor's Tricks

A Story Collection by

FuzzWolf

Illustrated by

Lapin Beau

Trevor's Tricks

Copyright © 2007 by FuzzWolf

Published by FurPlanet Productions.

All rights reserved.

ISBN: 978-1-935599-00-5

Printed in the United States of America

FurPlanet Productions
An imprint of Argyll Productions LLC
Dallas, TX

www.FurPlanet.com

Cover Art: Lapin Beau

For Teiran

And

My Mother, may she never read this!

TABLE OF CONTENTS

Preface

This book contains a selection of stories in the life of Trevor, the hot little fox whose initial shyness hides a writhing sea of horny kinkiness. These stories were written between 1999 and 2007 and were not written in the order they are presented here. Hopefully they hang together well enough to be enjoyed as one story despite being written out of order.

These tales were written to be something you could fap to, no more and no less. For the most part, I wrote about kinks I enjoyed and created characters I thought would be sexy and interesting. Originally I wrote these only for my own amusement, but I was gratified to discover that others enjoyed the stories too and were gracious enough to let me know how much.

I hope you find my characters appealing and my stories arousing. If my stories help you get off, then my work has lived up to its goal. Now, without further delay, here is what's in store for you:

Constant and graphic homosexual sex, anal, oral, domination, submission, spanking, cross-dressing, rimming, 3ways, public sex, predator and prey games, masturbation, knot play, rough sex, toys and completely shameless stereotypical wolf on fox action!

Acknowledgements

I'd just like to thank a few people who helped create this dead-tree (or futuristic virtual representation thereof) version my stories.

Teiran: If there's any romance in amongst all this porn, it's because of you. Thanks for being there for me. Its funny how often people mix up our stories so for everyone reading this, buy my mate's book, "The Hero" too!

Lapin Beau: I was really late getting Lapin the descriptions of the various scenes he was illustrating for this book, but he still managed to churn out eight drawings in time to have this printed. Thanks for working so hard on the interior illustrations as well as the magnificently gay cover.

E-mail Lapin at lapin_beau@yahoo.com Commission this artist! He's good and he's fast.

Tak: You worked yourself to the bone finishing Ringtail Café #3 in time for the deadline, but still offered to help me with my book cover. Thanks so much, I really appreciate the time you put in to help me out. I know your eyes will be scarred if you ever read the stories in this book, but I hope you see this part at least.

Please go to www.RingtailCafe.com to find out about the comic Tak writes with my friend Growly and his mate, Snowy. Keep an eye out for Fuzz's evil alter-ego, Zuff.

Alex Vance: Thanks for using your mad design skills to lay out this book for printing and being so flexible in dealing with us to get this venture off the ground.

Alex publishes furry books, please visit BadDogBooks.com and support more furry writing!

Thanks to all my real life furry friends. If I tried to list you all I'd forget someone and I wouldn't want to do that. My time spent in the furry community has been wonderful because of all of you.

I'd also to thank all the furs out there who have read any of my stories and taken the time to e-mail me or comment on YiffStar. All the positive feedback inspires me to keep writing. I read them all even if I don't always have time to reply. Don't stop e-mailing me; your comments are always appreciated.

And last, but not least. Thank you to all the wonderful furries I've slept with. Some of the tales in this book are based on real events that were just too hot not to commit to memory in some way. Thanks for the inspiration.

Sexual Predator

The heat in the club was almost stifling, the music was too loud, and most of the furs there were a bit skanky. Ray sighed and sipped his drink, surveying the crowd from the small back bar. The room was dominated by the stage in the center where the fetish show staff was setting up for the next act. Most furs were dancing in typical Goth fashion in front of the stage, but the big wolf was eyeing some of the wallflowers clustered off to the side. That was what he was looking for, one of the shyer types. In his experience, the shy ones were the best. Most of them repressed a great ocean of sexual energy waiting to explode, but were too unsure of themselves to really exploit that. That meant they were great for a passionate time, and were less likely to be germ-riddled than the more slutty types that were attractive and knew it. Now, what flavour was he in the mood for tonight, rabbit, cat, or maybe a little...

Ray smiled, sharp predatory teeth gleaming as he spied a likely candidate for some fun. On the other side of the stage, huddled in a dark spot by himself, was a fox. Focusing in on the fox, Ray took a deep sniff in the air. Through the haze of sweaty, furry bodies the fox's musk came through strong. The scent of male fox was unmistakable. Foxes almost always smelled like pure sex, even if they were virgins. Something about a fox always brought on the arousal of other furs, particularly the predator species, and this one was no different.

The wolf watched the fox's movements from across the room for a while. He was a short male, no more than five and half feet tall, perhaps a couple inches less. He was very fit looking though, not buffed out to grotesque proportions but he definitely worked out. His perfectly toned chest and stomach could be seen nicely through his black mesh shirt. The black leather collar he wore stood out brightly against the white fur of his throat, and matched his tight leather pants. The thing that caught Ray's wandering eye was the rather impressive and delicious looking lump in the fox's pants. Ray licked his lips a bit. For a male of such small stature the fox was obviously very well endowed. Pity he had that 'I've been dragged here by a friend' look about him. It was so typical of a fur as hot as this to not find himself attractive and feel out of place in a club like this. Ray decided he'd just have to introduce himself.

He began to make his way over when the little fox noticed him. Upon seeing the six-foot wolf who smelled of arousal heading in his direction, the shy fur got more than a little worried as to his intentions. He began to make his way toward the back door, slowly slipping between some of the bystanders who were now watching a black cat having candle wax poured on his nipples up on the stage. Ray grinned, the hunt was on. He pushed his way gently past the furs who were raptly watching the stage, getting ever closer to his target.

Trevor Fox gasped as the cool night air hit his face. He hadn't expected it to be so cool since he had been so used to the warmth of all the furry bodies inside the club. He stepped past the three or four furs standing outside the back door to smoke, and quickly descended the small set of crumbling concrete steps to the ground. He didn't see the wolf at the door yet and thought he may have lost him. Calming a little, he took a moment to look around the outside area of the club.

The place was actually pretty amazing. The area was about the size of an average house's back yard. All the plants were completely overgrowing, and the cobblestone path was broken in places with grass growing through the cracks. Benches and sofas were scattered around, some with furry bodies on them, either snuggling together or passing something that wasn't tobacco between them. Trevor wandered to what he hoped would be a quiet corner to sit for a bit and collect himself. He found a mostly-intact and dry concrete bench to sit on. He started to think he was over-reacting. He had no idea if the wolf he had seen had meant him any harm or not. Maybe he just wanted to talk or something. 'He was probably interested in me and I blew it', Trevor thought to himself. Upon reflection, when he wasn't scaring the hell out of him, the wolf hadn't been a bad looker. And those eyes had really caught his attention. They had almost glowed with a beautiful shade of green. Trevor smiled as he thought about it. The little fox was becoming more relaxed now. The woodsy smell of the overgrowing plants and trees around him probably helped that. If he closed his eyes he could imagine he was in a forest somewhere, back in the wild.

"Gotcha." A husky voice broke Trevor's train of thought as he felt strong paws grip his upper arms.

Trevor gasped; the wolf had found him after all. He hadn't been able to smell him with the strong scents of the undergrowth all around him. The wolf had stayed downwind and snuck around behind him. He whimpered a little as the wolf's large paws roamed over his body, caressing his chest and belly. Ray sat down around Trevor, holding the fox securely between his legs.

"You know what happens to foxes who get caught by wolves?" Ray rasped into the fox's trembling ear.

Trevor only whimpered in response, afraid for his life again.

"They get eaten." The wolf replied to his own question as he quickly brought his muzzle down on Trevor's neck, giving him a sharp nip.

Trevor yelped and tried to jump, but he was held fast in Ray's arms. The small fox weakly tried to struggle. He trembled; he knew what the wolf wanted. He looked down to see the wolf's legs were bare, off to the side he could see a small pile of clothes laying next to a nearby tree. That meant the hard lump he felt pressing against him was…

"P-please let me go." He squeaked.

"Now now, you don't dress like this…" Ray's left paw slid down Trevor's tight leather pants to squeeze the bulge of his foxhood. "If you only wanted to wallflower and spend the night alone."

Ray continued to rub up and down on the hardening lump at Trevor's crotch. Involuntarily, Trevor's legs parted just enough to allow Ray to reach between his thighs to give a gentle squeeze where his balls were. Trevor whimpered.

"Feels to me like at least one part of you likes all this attention." Ray rubbed a bit more vigorously now, his paw heated up as it rubbed against the leather. He could feel the foxhood stirring beneath, feeling like it needed to be released.

"I'll let you go anytime you want, but I know you want this." Ray gave the lump a firm squeeze.

"Oh…oh gods," Trevor gasped, unable to control himself any longer. His raging hormones were making his blood boil, and he couldn't deny his own nature any longer. He was a fox, and he was made to fuck. He moaned as he was groped and squeezed, his cock ached to be released from the tight prison of his pants. "yes" he squeaked. And that was all that needed to be said.

While holding Trevor firmly with his left paw, Ray reached between them to undo the catch above Trevor's tail. He switched paws to undo the lacings along the front of the fox's pants. Trevor wiggled a bit as Ray helped his pants to slip off. Ray looked and grinned as he noticed Trevor wore no underwear.

"You really did want this tonight, didn't you naughty fox," he said, taking a firm hold of Trevor's dripping erection.

The fox moaned out a long "Yeessssss" in response. Ray continued to stroke the foxhood firmly in long and slow strokes. He looked in amazement at the fox's endowment. He didn't want to admit it, but if not for his knot, it would be bigger than his own. It was already thicker, but the fox didn't need to know that.

"Now, lift your tail for me fox." Ray commanded, fully in control.

Trevor obeyed, hesitating just a bit as he lifted his bushy tail, leaving his tailhole vulnerable and exposed. His rational mind screamed at him for submitting so completely to a stranger. It also reminded him that out here they didn't have any kind of lubricant, and he had no idea how big this wolf was. But his other side, his instincts, kicked in and he knew he really, really needed this. He looked across the yard to see a dozen eyes watching him as the wolf slowly lifted his body. Some watched from the corners of their eyes as they went down on each other, and at least one or two were watching him intently as they passed a joint between them while pawing themselves off. 'I'm about to get fucked in public' was Trevor's last thought before he felt the wolf's hard cockhead against his pucker.

Ray pulled the fox down, groaning as he felt the familiar tight warmth of a tailhole gripping his cock.

Trevor's mouth opened in pain, but no sound came out as the wolfcock, lubed with only a drop or two of precum, opened him up and penetrated his insides. The wolf didn't wait for the pain to subside before he began moving Trevor up and down on his lap, allowing his wolfhood to pump in and out of Trevor's twitching hole.

By the fifth or sixth inward thrust, the pain had begun to be replaced with pleasure. Trevor began moaning, his head thrown back, eyes closed. His cock streamed precum as he was deeply penetrated over and over. His arms moved freely for a moment, not sure what to hold onto to steady himself. That was when his wolf captor stood up, still gripping him tightly about the waist. He was turned around and bent over the concrete bench he had been sitting on. The wolf forced his legs fully apart with one foot, and held him down with two strong paws on his back. Now fully in a position of power over him, the wolf began to really hump into him hard and fast. Trevor's body rocked with the force of the intense fucking, he squealed a little after a particularly deep thrust.

Ray was really enjoying himself now, the little fox was a lot tighter than he had thought he'd be. He gloried in the power of being on top, proving to the smaller fur who the more dominant male was in this situation. His knot had begun to form, thickening quickly and popping in and out of the fox's stretched anus. He could feel the pressure of impending orgasm beginning to build up, starting deep in his balls and moving up to the base of his cock.

"Oh, gods, yes" he muttered, his thrusting becoming more erratic now. He could feel it more and more now, it was so very close. Any moment now he would pop his knot into his prey a final time, locking them together, and he would cum deep inside the fox's body. So close now…so close the pleasure was almost overwhelming. The pressure continued to build, almost unbearably. The release of orgasm would be so welcome. 'Here it comes,' he thought, just one more thrust…

A firm paw grabbed Ray's shoulder and pulled back. He fell back, his long cock pulling out of Trevor's body. Trevor gasped loudly as the whole cock was removed from him so suddenly. He turned around to see what was happening; surely the wolf wouldn't have let him go before finishing with him.

When he turned he saw that the wolf he had previously thought was very physically imposing, was now being held around the neck by a much larger wolf. Trevor sat back, watching, wondering what was going to happen now.

The newcomer was huge, well over six feet tall and built. He obviously worked out. His fur was all iron gray in colour except for a little red around his muzzle.

"Ray," he grunted. "I thought I told you it wasn't nice to take advantage of smaller furs."

Ray was almost in a haze, the pressure in his balls hadn't been released and was now approaching painful. He'd run into this wolf before, he somehow thought it wasn't fair to use one's natural dominance to get what one wanted despite that being the way things were done.

"Sinclair, you son of a bitch!" he snarled. "I wasn't doing anything wrong, and look at him. He even liked it."

They both looked over at Trevor. The small fox blushed under his fur, unable to hide his rather large and dripping erection in time.

"Nothing wrong, eh. Then you won't mind if I do… this" Sinclair roughly pulled Ray's tail out of the way, and in one quick move he had bent him over and shoved his own eight inch wolfhood into Ray's tailhole.

Ray cried out, half in anger and half at the pain of the sudden intrusion. He fell forward, holding himself up with his forepaws on the stone bench. He was in the same position Trevor had been in only moments before. His painfully hard cock dripped precum onto the ground beneath him.

Sinclair stood up behind him, stroking his back.

"Hmm, you know I could grow to like this." He chuckled.

He slipped a paw underneath Ray to tickle and squeeze his balls, knowing how much the other wolf needed to cum. Ray whimpered loudly. He didn't know what was worse, being mounted forcefully by the more dominant wolf, or that his poor balls ached and needed release so badly.

Sinclair looked over to where Trevor sat staring.

"Hey, little guy you look like you're pretty randy yerself. Tell you what," He began to hump Ray as he spoke "Once I'm done with him, you can have a go. I'll loosen him up for you, how's that sound?"

Trevor grinned for a moment before catching the glare from Ray. He gulped. "Um, that sounds… uh, sure."

Sinclair smiled back, continuing to hump the squirming wolf beneath him. "Well, I'm Sinclair. Nice to meet you."

Trevor couldn't help returning the big wolf's friendly smile as he introduced himself, "Name's Trevor."

Sinclair winked at him before returning all his attention to the task at hand. He gripped Ray's sides tightly and leaned into him, now pushing his whole, hard length into the once-dominant wolf. He knew what Ray found so attractive about being so in control, but he preferred to do it with a willing fur. As he felt his knot beginning to swell and the pressure of his cum building up, Sinclair slipped one paw between his thrusting thighs and his prey's body so as to keep his knot from locking the two together. He didn't want to be tied to Ray; he still had to allow

Trevor to have his fun too.

Ray snarled and whimpered at the relentless pounding, feeling the more dominant male's cock beginning to thicken as he approached release. Sinclair rocked his body back and forth as his thrusts came quicker. Sinclair squeezed his own knot tightly at the apex of his pleasure, which caused him to cum hard. He groaned out loud as he felt the wonderful release, shooting his cum deep inside the wolf's hot body.

"Oh, gods yeah." Sinclair sighed, thrusting while squeezing his knot one last time. He looked over to where Trevor was raptly watching them. "Ready for your turn little guy?"

Trevor nodded eagerly, still watching intently as Sinclair pulled his spent cock from under Ray's limp tail. The little fox was still quite nervous and hanging back just a bit.

"Its okay Trevor, don't be afraid." Sinclair held his hand out.

Trevor gently took it and allowed himself to be led over to where Sinclair stood. The physically imposing, but very kind wolf lifted his beaten foe's tail to reveal the dripping pucker that waited there.

Trevor's cock glistened with precum as he got closer. He looked up with almost child-like eyes at Sinclair.

"I've...never done this before." He confessed, blushing a bit under his red fur.

"Sssh, its alright sweet fox, I'll help you." Sinclair pulled the nervous little fox around so he stood between the two wolves. He held Trevor close so the fox felt safe and secure in the big wolf's arms. All of a sudden Ray didn't seem that big or strong any more. Trevor began to feel more confident as he looked at the wolf who had previously hunted him. Ray now looked back at the two furs with a pitiful look, not sure if he could take another right now; especially another fairly large one like what he'd seen on that little fox earlier.

Sinclair walked forward, nudging Trevor gently along as he went. Trevor gulped a bit as his cocktip brushed against the fur between Ray's cheeks. He let out a long breath once his tip was against the wolf's tail hole. It already felt warm against his sensitive tip, and was moist from Sinclair's cum which had dribbled out a little. Sinclair leaned close to Trevor, bringing his muzzle against one little fox ear.

"Now, just push forward." He said, his voice soft and smooth. He placed his hands on Trevor's smallish, perfectly round butt and helped him along by gently pushing him forward.

Ray squeaked a bit as the thick foxcock entered him. Trevor moaned as Sinclair continued to push him forward, the hot tailhole swallowing up his foxhood. Sinclair stopped pushing and held Trevor close, hugging him, once he was fully embedded inside Ray's tight tailhole. He held him for a moment before standing off to the side.

"Now, fuck him." He commanded.

Trevor obeyed the authority in Sinclair's voice without question. He began to do as he was told, moving his hips back and forth slowly at first, his thick maleness opened up the wolf even more than before.

Sinclair smiled as he saw the look of pleasure on the little fox's face as he humped his would-be predator. He walked around to where Ray's face lay. The beaten wolf was beginning to look a bit like he was spacing out, trying to be somewhere else. Sinclair rubbed his cock against Ray's muzzle. His cock still dripped a little cum.

"Clean it," He ordered.

Ray tried to snarl in disgust for a moment before Sinclair forced his muzzle open with his paws and shoved his dripping member past his lips. The smaller wolf gagged a little before relenting to his situation and beginning to lick and suck at

Sinclair's cock.

Sinclair hadn't meant for the other wolf to give him a blowjob, but it seemed to be turning out that way. It just felt too good so he stayed with it, letting Ray lick and suck him all he wanted. He looked over to see Trevor now thoroughly enjoying himself on Ray's other end. He was putting all his foxy sexuality into the act and was now tightly gripping the fur of Ray's back as his hips thrust rapidly. He pounded into the wolf's stretched anus like an animal possessed. Sinclair decided it would be fun to really give it to Ray from both ends. He began to thrust his cock back and forth in the sucking muzzle. Ray gagged for a moment before getting into the rhythm as Sinclair muzzle-fucked him.

Meanwhile, Trevor could not believe what he had been missing all this time. He thought he had loved to be dominated and fucked, but he had no idea how good being on top felt. He felt in control, powerful, and the heat and pressure on his cock was the most intense pleasure he had ever felt. He knew he couldn't last much longer. His speed increased again, determined to cum hard inside this wolf now. His looked down in awe as his thick maleness disappeared again and again under the wolf's bushy tail. He wondered if this was what he looked like while being fucked. Watching something that thick penetrate a hole that small was truly fascinating to him.

Sinclair wondered what Trevor was so intent on watching even as they both kept up a speedy rhythm. Sinclair looked down to concentrate on driving his cock into Ray's muzzle. He could only do that for a few moments however when his attention was grabbed by an almost painful sounding shout. He looked up to see Trevor's small body rigidly straight and quivering all over as he shot his load deep inside their shared wolf. He smiled as he saw the look of rapturous pleasure on the fox's face as he came.

Trevor thrust hard and deep three or four more times as he

emptied his balls fully. He milked that orgasm as long as he could. It was the most powerful he had ever felt, and he thought the force of it was going to make him pass out. He pushed himself up, balancing his weight on Ray's back.

Sinclair smiled over to him.

"All done over there?"

Trevor could only nod and brace himself for the pain/pleasure on his over-sensitive organ as he pulled out slowly. Ray whimpered around his mouthful of cock as he felt the thick foxhood drag its way out of him slowly.

Sinclair continued to hump his wolfhood into Ray's muzzle as he spoke.

"Think this one has learned his lesson yet?" He grinned back at Trevor.

Trevor looked down at the thoroughly beaten and submissive wolf, and decided to take some pity on him. He looked underneath Ray to see the wolf's poor neglected cock, now beginning to soften a bit. He could see the wolf's balls were significantly swollen, full of cum just begging to be released. He began to softly paw the wolf's tender ballsack, eliciting a painful little whimper from Ray as he did. He looked up at Sinclair.

"I think he has."

Sinclair smiled at the fox, seeing how softhearted and kind the little fur was.

Trevor got an idea for how he'd like to help the poor wolf finally get some relief. He was so turned on now from all that had happened that he didn't want to stop yet anyway.

"Let him up." He told Sinclair, who complied silently, letting the little fox have the show now.

Sinclair pulled his throbbing wolfhood from Ray's tired muzzle and waited for Trevor's next move. Trevor made an indication of what he wanted to do, so Sinclair helped him flip Ray over onto his back so that he was now lying on the stone bench. At this point, Ray was too tired and submissive to really care. He let this pair do whatever they wanted with him now.

With a mischievous foxy grin on his muzzle, Trevor climbed up onto the bench, coming up between Ray's legs. He started by gently licking the sensitive spot between Ray's furry sack and tail hole. Ray tried to stifle a little moan as Trevor continued to move up, licking and sucking on the wolf's full balls. Trevor smiled as he saw Ray's cock had begun to stir and harden again. He let a swollen wolfball drop from his muzzle as he moved onto his next target, Ray's dripping cock.

Sinclair looked on with interest as Trevor licked and sucked Ray's wolfhood to full hardness again. He smiled as he saw what the fox had in mind when Trevor pulled his muzzle off of Ray's cock to leave it very wet, dripping with saliva.

Trevor moved up Ray's body, crouching over him. He shuddered a little as he felt the wolf's hard cockhead rub past his hanging balls. He looked down into the wolf's half curious, half frightened eyes as he took the dripping cock gently in his soft paw and placed it at his tailhole. With a smile and a wink he slid back, allowing the slick wolfcock to penetrate him.

Ray moaned and involuntarily thrust upwards, hilting himself the rest of the way in the little fox. This got a pleasurable squeal from Trevor as his recently used prostate got a nice bump from Ray's cock. He decided to give the wolf a little something back for that by squeezing his anal muscles down as hard as he could, causing Ray to buck and moan beneath him. Now Trevor began moving up and down the long wolfcock, riding him slowly.

Sinclair looked on for a bit longer before realizing that watching the pair in action was causing his already hard cock to throb painfully. He cocked his head as he continued to watch, deciding whether to join in or not. His paw moved by itself to begin slowly stroking himself. He moved around behind the other furs, his paw still slowly working his thick cock as he did. He leaned down between Ray's spread legs and moved his muzzle forward till he could see the point where Ray's cock spread open the small fox's tailhole. Extending his long wolf tongue, Sinclair began to lick both males here. He lapped at the base of Ray's wolfhood, then moved up to rim Trevor's stretched hole. Both furs moaned and gasped at the additional sensation as they kept up their movement, Trevor was now fiercely riding the wolfhood that was deep inside him. Smiling at the reaction, Sinclair moved down again to lick Ray's full balls. His tongue bounced the white-furred sac up and down, lapping the wolf's swollen balls that were so badly in need of release. At this point, Ray's knot had swollen up rather quickly. It was now fully hard, and Trevor's hole bumped against it on each downward stroke. Seeing this, Sinclair held Ray's furry thighs down and began to lick and suck at his knot. This was not only very stimulating for the wolf, but allowed Sinclair to make sure Ray would not tie with Trevor and risk hurting the little fox again. He was surprised that he was really starting to care about the submissive fox.

Trevor grunted and gasped, Ray's cock had thickened more inside him and he could tell the wolf was not far from finally cumming. He was still quite horny himself between the really great experience he'd just had in topping and all the prodding that was happening to his prostate right now. He was creating a good rhythm with stroking his foxhood, which had grown to full hardness again, and riding the hard wolfcock under his tail. The feeling was really overwhelming as he was in control to ride it at his own pace, and use Ray for his own pleasure in a slightly different way.

Below them, Sinclair's cock demanded attention again. He decided to grip Ray's cock at the base to hold it down with one paw so he could paw himself off with the other. He continued to lick and nibble at the soft fur on Ray's ball sac as he frantically worked his thick, hard wolfhood.

After several more minutes of riding, squeezing, pawing, and licking, the first one went off. Sinclair gasped loudly as cum fired from his thick tip, coating his paws in white streams of wolfseed. As he came, he clenched down on Ray's knot, holding it tightly. This was what finally put Ray over the edge. The wolf almost passed out as he came at last. The orgasm was over-powering. He shot two loads worth of cum at once since he had already been forced to suppress a near orgasm earlier. He filled the little fox so much he could feel it dribble back down his shaft and over his knot. Naturally, being filled to the point of bursting with wolf cum brought on Trevor's orgasm too. He shuddered and gasped as his fox cream shot from his overly sensitive organ. He couldn't stop himself though, he kept stroking till his balls were empty again and he had coated parts of Ray's chest with his load.

After a few minutes of panting and trying to regain some strength, the three spent furs separated from each other. They looked around to see that all around them, cocks were spurting and cum was flying in all directions. They smiled, seeing the effect they'd had on the voyeur crowd around them.

They exchanged pleasantries and went their separate ways for the night. They all agreed that despite the darker beginnings they had all had a great evening out, and they had all learned something new.

Trevor had learned he did indeed find it arousing to be taken forcefully, but also how wonderful topping was. He endeavored to do that again.

Ray learned that being taken in the tail hole isn't has bad as he thought it would be, and despite wanting to be the alpha male he secretly wanted to be taken like that again.

Sinclair could only smile and hope to see the two furs again. He'd discovered that watching was quite arousing too.

Although they went their separate ways, they exchanged numbers and made plans to see each other again.

Something I Can Never Have

T revor cast his bleary eyes to the car's clock for the third
time in the last fifteen minutes.

3:35 AM

He sighed and shut off the radio. He was nervous about going
into his apartment because he knew his roommate would still be
up. He'd never come home this late before, and he'd never come
home from a night like tonight before either. He figured he might
was well get this over with, and got out of the car. He caught his
reflection in the rear-view mirror as he stood. He realized he didn't
look half-bad, and for the first time in his life he thought he could
see what someone would see in him.

When at his apartment door, he turned the key very slowly so as
to make as little noise as possible. The fox slipped inside and shut
the door quietly. He got about halfway through the living room
before his roommate commented.

"You're home late, Trev."

Trevor gulped; at least Lewis hadn't turned around. The short,
slightly pudgy wolf's eyes were still fixed on the computer screen.

From here, Trevor couldn't tell if he was working on homework or just surfing the net.

"Um, yeah guess so," he mumbled, not quite sure what to say.

The hesitancy in his voice was what got Lewis' attention. The little wolf turned around slowly, his eyes going big as they took in his vulpine roommate.

He didn't know what was more surprising. He'd never seen Trevor wear anything quite like what he had on now. The fox was wearing the tightest leather pants Lewis had ever seen; they showed off every curve of the fox's trim body. The tight, mesh shirt showed off Trevor's chest very nicely, and the leather collar stood in stark contrast to the white fur of his throat. More than the outfit though, Lewis was struck by how... rumpled the fox appeared. His headfur was a mess, his face looked dirty, and his tail was very untidy. For Trevor, having his tail's fur not perfectly groomed was really odd.

Lewis set his reading glasses down on his mouse pad and stood up.

"Trevor, what happened to you?"

Trevor sagged a bit, and made his way to sit down on the couch. Inside, he had been wondering what to tell Lewis. He could have been evasive and just run off to his room, but it'd be so obvious that tonight had not been a normal night out. Trevor had worn this outfit before, but he always left before Lewis came home from class, and returned early in the evening because nothing ever happened. Usually when he came home, Lewis had gone back out to the library or the computer lab.

In the end, Trevor decided to tell Lewis all about his night. He needed someone to talk to about a night this amazing. It might as well be his roommate. The two had become good friends in the last year, although they still didn't really know very much about each other.

Lewis joined Trevor on the couch, and sat in rapt attention as the fox told him of a night of being hunted, rescued by a real hunk of a wolf, and lust-filled sex. The wolf shifted uncomfortably on the couch as his sheath filled with arousal at the tale. He'd always thought Trevor was a rather shy type. He had no idea he was capable of displaying this much sexuality, in either his dress or his actions.

When he was finished, Trevor stood up. "I'm going to bed now. I don't know if I'll be able to sleep though. Wheeee," he giggled, "I'm still so excited. I can't believe this happened to me."

Lewis had to smile a bit at his friend's enthusiasm even though he ached inside.

"Um, are you going to call them?"

Trevor stopped, and pulled out the two little pieces of paper in the pocket of his tight pants. He had two phone numbers because the three of them had agreed to exchange numbers. He was only interested in one though, his handsome rescuer. He looked at Sinclair's messy paw writing and smiled with the memory of the gentle giant.

"Yeah, I'm going to call one of them."

Trevor turned to go to his room and Lewis asked him.

"Love…or something like it?"

The fox stopped and thought.

"I don't know yet. All I know is, he was really sweet to me, and I definitely want to see him again."

"Ah," Lewis said with a smile.

Trevor smiled back and made his way to his room.

When Lewis heard the door shut behind the fox, he sighed. He sat up a little bit and slipped his shorts down. He pushed them down to his ankles, and then leaned back again. He looked at the hard, canine cock sticking up from his sheath, half obscured by his little, round belly. Trevor's story had really gotten to him, in more ways than one. He looked around for a minute, a little worried about doing this in the living room. He figured he was pretty safe from being disturbed. Trevor was his only roommate, and he'd most likely be in his room a while even if he didn't go to sleep.

With a stifled whimper, Lewis took hold of his wolfhood. He gently ran his fingertips over its surface; it throbbed under his touch as he teased himself. He wrapped his paw around his shaft and began to slowly slide it up and down. He didn't grip yet; he loved to feel a gentle stroking on his member for now. He softly stroked at himself, whimpering softly, his tail trying to wag against the couch making him shift his rump about. He reached down with his other paw and began to fondle his full balls. It had been some time since he'd pawed off, and his balls ached with need now. He gasped as he gave his balls a little squeeze.

He lay there for several minutes, just stroking and squeezing himself gently. The young wolf closed his eyes and let his head rest against the soft pillows of the old couch. His mind started to wander to his beautiful roommate. In his mind, Trevor came out of his room to be with him. He left the wolf who had so impressed him behind on the computer to pay attention to Lewis instead. Lewis whimpered as he imagined the scene. He could see it so clearly as he slowly ran his soft-furred paw up and down his shaft.

In his mind, Lewis saw Trevor walking across the living room toward him. The fox's perfect form was outlined in the half-light from his bedroom door. Lucky for the fantasizing wolf, he knew exactly what the object of his desire looked like naked. He had accidentally walked in on Trevor pawing off one day when the hapless fox had forgotten to lock his door. For a precious few seconds, Lewis had gotten a full view of what the pretty fox looked like in the throes of passion. Of course, Trevor had been painfully embarrassed and instantly hid himself with a thick blanket. The fox had held a special place in Lewis' heart for some time before that, and now he had fueled that even more by getting to the wolf on a very primal level as well.

The wolf could see perfectly in his rampant imagination. Trevor walked across the room to Lewis' side, oohing as he watched his cuddly roommate masturbate. Lewis licked his lips as he carefully watched the fox's plump sheath. The vulpine pawed himself to full hardness as he stepped between Lewis' parted legs. He leaned down close to Lewis, his furry cheek tickling the wolf's ear a bit as he whispered, "I love you, my sexy wolf."

The lusty figment's paws roamed over Lewis' chest, tweaking his nipples then caressing his soft, ample belly. Lewis whimpered as Trevor teased him in his mind. The little wolf squeezed his eyes shut for a second as he slowly ran his fingertips over the crown of his cockhead.

Sometimes he thought about how much he'd love the beautiful fox to make love to him, slowly and romantically. Then there were other times, like now, when he was so turned on and pent up. As he imagined Trevor rubbing his wonderful, thick cockhead under his balls, he begged Trevor in a whisper to mount him hard and cum inside him.

"As you wish, sexy boy," Trevor whispered in his ear.

Lewis stroked his shaft up and down; achingly slow, as he wanted this to last. He moved one paw between his legs, his fingers moved towards his tailhole as he imagined Trevor's perfect cockhead pressing against his tight anal ring. His little belly jiggled a little as he lifted his legs up to press his fingers against his opening. His tail wriggled in excitement against the couch as he took a deep breath.

The fantasy fox drove his long, thick cock deep inside the

FuzzWolf

quivering wolf. Lewis could not fully suppress a slight cry as he thought of the solid foxmeat opening him up. He bit down to keep from whimpering too loud as the pain of being spread open radiated from under his tail, and was then replaced with extreme pleasure as he touched himself deep inside. Lewis' wolfhood drooled precum as he pressed against his prostate and slowly stroked himself.

The wolf quivered and shook as he thought of Trevor violently humping him. He could almost feel Trev's thick, eight inches pounding into him, opening him up again and again.

"Ohhh, fuck," Lewis cried out as he came.

The gray wolf's short, chubby cock spurted hard, sending a thick stream of wolfseed over his shoulder. The next few spurts were progressively less powerful, but coated the canid's chest and belly in sticky cum.

Lewis panted for several seconds, still holding his limp cock in one paw as the fingers of his other paw slipped from his self-ravaged ass. He almost forgot he wasn't safe in his room as he stretched and enjoyed the afterglow until…

"Wow, that was cool."

Lewis sat bolt upright, his eyes locking with those of his roommate.

Trevor was standing there, watching in amazement. He was wearing only his thin boxers, and he was very obviously aroused.

"I mean, I've never been able to cum so hard by pawing myself. That looked awesome!"

Trevor grinned wildly, obviously enthusiastic to discover his roommate was a sexual being after all. Up until now, he'd wondered if the little wolf only used his cock to relieve himself.

"I-I-I," Lewis stuttered, jumping off the couch and pulling his shorts back up over his sticky crotch.

Trevor walked towards him, reaching out to hug him, tell-

31

ing him it was okay, everybody did it. Lewis panicked. He didn't know how long Trevor had been standing there, he didn't know if he had seen him using his fingers on himself, and worst of all, he didn't know if Trevor had heard him beg to be mounted by him. He blushed furiously, and just as the fox was about to hug him and comfort him, Lewis bolted. Trevor almost fell over as the frantic wolf ran for the safety of his room.

Once inside, he slammed and locked the door. He fell against the closed door, tears streaming down his muzzle. He could hear Trevor pawing gently at the door. His canine ears couldn't block out the sound of his soft and sweet voice, so full of concern.

"I'm sorry Lewis. I didn't mean to scare you... please come out?"

"Just leave me alone," Lewis moaned then threw himself into bed. He covered his head with blankets and pillows, trying to drown out the world and what had just happened.

Outside the locked bedroom door, Trevor sighed. He didn't know what to do or say in this situation. He was never good at comforting people, as he had so rarely been comforted himself. He thought maybe if Lewis really wanted to be alone now, he shouldn't push him to talk.

The fox's tail drooped as he went back to his own room.

He sighed, sitting down in front of his computer to say goodnight to his new friend.

Sinclair >>   *Trevor?*

Sinclair >>   *Everything all right?*

TrevFox >>   *I don't know…*

Something I Can Never Have

Some Like it Rough

"Hey Lewis.

This is gonna seem like a weird request. Tonight is the night I'm meeting a fur at the Dewdrop Inn for some fun like I told you about.

I just wanted to let someone I trust know where I am and what I'll be doing just in case anything should happen.

I'm pretty nervous<g>, but I think this is a part of me I should really explore. I'm attaching a file with all the info I have on the guy, and the number and address of where I'll be.

Thanks for watching my back buddy. I'll take you out sometime to make up for this. :-)

Your pal,
Trevor"

ATTACHEMENT

Lewis gulped a little as he read his e-mail. He knew his friend Trevor had a lot of kinks that he was beginning to explore, and he was worried for him. He only hoped his friend, who was maybe a bit too trusting, was safe and knew what he was doing.

"I hope they're meeting in a public place at least," Lewis muttered to himself...

"I should have insisted on a more public place," Trevor half-whimpered to himself as he pulled his car into the rather beat-up looking parking lot of the hotel he and his rendezvous had agreed on.

The young fox leaned his head back and sighed deeply. He was nervous. He looked over at the lobby; its bright light looked welcoming and safe, but still somewhat unsettling.

'This is it', he thought. He had to go get the room now, then wait for the inevitable. Trevor gathered up his courage and stepped out of the car, making the short walk to the lobby.

The middle-aged shrew behind the counter gave Trevor a long look up and down as he entered. Trevor could see in her eyes she knew exactly what he was here for. He wondered if it was in the way he was dressed, or just his nervous manner. Truthfully, it was just that kind of motel, and she'd seen a lot weirder than this shaky looking young fox in his tight, leather pants.

Trevor was even nervous about getting the room, especially since it was all too obvious what he was going to be using it for. He'd always thought of himself as a pretty clean-living fur, and now he felt a little dirty about getting a room for this. At least he wasn't hiring a prostitute, he thought and felt a little better. The clerk barely spoke as she checked him in and handed him a room key.

"Thanks," he mumbled and quickly made his way back to his car, nearly tripping over his feet.

Once in his room, he tossed his jacket over one of the chairs around the little table near the door. He used the restroom, adjusted his fur several times and paced a bit before he decided the pacing was making him feel worse and he settled onto a bed to call Sinclair as he had promised. With a shaking paw, he made the phone call to Sinclair to tell him the room number he was in. The conversation was short and to the point. The wolf said he'd be on his way in a moment.

He still had thirty minutes before their scheduled time to meet so he tried to be as comfortable as possible in the meantime, and so he settled back down onto the bed for now.

He reflected on how he had gotten here. He had first met Sinclair about a month ago on his first night out alone. He had gone to a neat looking Goth/S & M club downtown that he had seen advertised in the local gay guides. It was his first night there and he had been near-raped, but Sinclair had stepped in and the situation had turned out okay. In fact, it was a really new experience for him and he had really enjoyed exploring himself a little more. He had turned out to have a bit more top in him than he had thought previously, but knew he was still a submissive at heart just as Sinclair's calling had been to be more dominant.

At the time, he had seen Sinclair as his knight in shining armor who had stepped in and saved him. The two had started talking over e-mail about their various interests, and now he was here.

One of Trevor's big kinks was spanking, and he blushed at the mere thought of that. It was a little embarrassing for him to talk about, and it had taken a lot of trust to even bring up the topic with Sinclair. The big wolf had asked him what his interests were, and what he'd like to try and explore that he hadn't much of a chance to yet. Trevor had taken this opportunity and bore some of his desires. They had discussed many fantasies and kinks they had interest in over the course of the last month, and had eventually decided to meet again in the fur. They had agreed on a little spanking fun.

The hardest part had been done now. Trevor had opened up and talked about his hidden desires that he'd held a long time with no outlet. Once that part was over, the next couple of e-mails had flowed easily. The time and the place had been agreed on quickly, and now the night had arrived.

Trevor thought he'd been safe, but still had lingering doubts. He trusted Sinclair after the night at the club, and he seemed sincere in his e-mails, but how much did he really know him. He had even taken the wise precaution of telling a close friend exactly what he was doing and who he was going to be with. That alone was quite embarrassing, but Lewis was a friend whom he cared about and found he could trust. Lewis wouldn't make fun of him about this, and he'd be there in case anything… bad should happen.

Trevor could see the sheen of his leather pants in the mirror, and he thought about the e-mails he and Sinclair had exchanged.

>>> *What should I wear?*

>> *::grins:: Definitely wear those yummy leather pants you wore to the club.*

> *Um, okay. What about, err underneath?*

::chuckles:: Doesn't matter to me, wear what you would like. You won't be wearing much for long anyway. :-)

On the top, Trevor had just chosen a regular t-shirt, white with the logo of an annual furry party on it. He looked over at the clock on the nightstand. Only fifteen minutes now. He stretched on the bed, spreading out to his full 5 foot 4 inch height. The slim fox suddenly jumped up and began to remove his shoes. He figured it was less to do later, and he liked to be fully prepared. It was also another way to kill a couple of minutes along with taking a sip from a glass of water and pacing the room another few times.

Twenty more minutes passed and he saw car lights just in front of his window. He instantly felt the butterflies rise up in his stomach. He could hear the driver's door slam shut, and the trunk open. He made his way slowly to the door; paw shaking as he reached for the door handle.

When the knock came, Trevor whipped open the door quickly. Sinclair stood there, his fist still raised at where the door had been.

Trevor was silent for a moment before squeaking out a "Hi" and going silent.

Sinclair smiled and stepped inside, holding a large suitcase. Trevor knew what was in there, all the implements the big wolf needed for a fun night. Sinclair firmly shut and locked the door behind him.

"Hi again, remembered to wear the pants, I see."

Trevor blushed and stepped back nervously as Sinclair set the case down in front of the bed. He popped it open and began to place several items on the edge of the bed.

"This should be enough to us started," Sinclair said as he looked back up at Trevor with a smile.

Trevor smiled back nervously, hoping the wolf wouldn't notice the bulge that had started to form in his tight pants.

"Nervous, huh?"

The fox just nodded. Inside he was half-terrified and half incredibly excited. He wanted this, or at least he thought he did. In his mind, his fantasies were always wonderful. He dreamed often of being bent over the knee of a big, strong male like Sinclair, but he still had the jitters. He hadn't been spanked like this before. He had no idea how it would feel in real life, and his mind was full of questions. 'What if it's not like I thought it would be?' 'What if this goes farther than I want to?' His biggest worry was disappointing his new friend. He worried that he wouldn't be able to take all that Sinclair could give, and the wolf would look down on him.

"It's okay foxy," Sinclair said as he stood up and approached Trevor.

He looked into the scared vulpine's eyes as he spoke, "I've been doing this a long time, and I can tell how much a boy can take. I won't go too fast, and I'll respect your limits. Do you trust me?"

Trevor had dropped his eyes for a second, feeling too scared and submissive to really look the imposing canine in the eye. He now looked back up, feeling slightly better now. He was still nervous as hell, but was ready to get to it. Whether it was a hurry to get it over with, or excitement, he couldn't quite tell.

"Yes," the fox almost whispered.

Sinclair leaned down and locked his muzzle with Trevor's. The fox melted in his arms as the deep kiss went on. Sinclair reached down and fondled the lump in the front of Trevor's pants. The fox moaned around Sinclair's muzzle as the wolf squeezed his trapped cock.

Now that Trevor appeared to be a bit more relaxed, Sinclair slowly pulled Trevor with him as he sat down at the foot of the bed. The big wolf was very gentle, even caressing the fox's face softly, as he slowly pulled Trevor over his knee. The fox sighed as he settled into the position he'd longed to be in since he was a kit.

Sinclair held the fox's back with one paw while slowly stroking his tail with his right paw. He stroked the bushy foxtail for several moments till Trevor relaxed even more. Now, Sinclair began to caress the fox's leather-clad rear. The tight pants outlined every curve of Trevor's ass perfectly. Sinclair could feel his sheath thicken at the sight of it, and the thought of plunging his cock under that lovely tail sprang into his mind. He dismissed it for now; perhaps later he'd have that chance.

Trevor knew the wolf was about ready when he felt the paw on his rear stop moving. Sinclair held it still against the lower curve of Trevor's rump. It was a comforting weight there. Sinclair gave Trevor a moderate tap with his palm. The fox jumped a bit out of instinct before realizing it didn't hurt at all. In fact, he could barely feel the wolf's paw through the leather.

Sinclair lightly slapped the leather-protected rear repeatedly with the same intensity. He alternated from the right to the left side, from just below the tail to the lower curve of the butt. He very slowly edged his way up a bit, and kept up the rhythm.

Trevor noticed the minor changed in intensity and cooed under his breath. He was starting to enjoy himself, and he was relieved that Sinclair was taking this so slowly and carefully.

Sinclair was a very astute observer of his spankees, and could tell the young fox was ready for a little more. He took the intensity of his slaps up another notch. His paw now made a much more audible slap against the leather each time. Trevor moaned a little, he could feel more now. The wolf's heavy palm felt great against his upturned rear. He could feel his cock throbbing against his pants again, and he realized he desperately wanted to feel Sinclair's strong paw against his bare fur.

The fox whimpered a bit as Sinclair began to spank him a bit harder again. This went on for several minutes as Sinclair gradually worked Trevor up to a relatively hard spanking. Trevor whimpered and bucked in Sinclair's lap. He could feel his butt beginning to get quite tender. His cock was fully hard now, painfully held prisoner in his clothes.

Sinclair stopped for a moment, and the pair breathed for a second. The wolf's heavy paw gently patted the warmed leather under Trevor's tail. With a grin, Sinclair undid the snap above the fox's tail. Trevor reached down and hastily undid the lacings at the front of his pants. His fingers worked with desperation until he could feel the leather waist become loose. Not a moment after he had undone the front; Sinclair began to pull his pants down. Trevor raised himself up a bit as the wolf pulled. He was ready now; Sinclair had warmed his butt and worked him up slowly. He badly needed to be spanked hard now.

"Oh my," Sinclair chuckled to himself.

Trevor blushed furiously. He had forgotten what he'd chosen to wear under his pants. He whimpered as the wolf's large paw gently caressed his rear through the thin panties he was wearing. He'd developed an interest in girl's underwear not long ago, and since Sinclair hadn't had a preference to what he wore tonight he figured he'd enjoy two kinks at once. Being spanked in panties was something he found very arousing. His cock throbbed with need, tenting the front of the thin panties and bumping against Sinclair's leg.

"Is it…okay?" Trevor asked in a timid voice.

Sinclair smiled as he continued to stroke the lacy, red panties that covered the fox's beautiful rump.

"It's perfect," he replied.

Trevor sighed in relief, and then gasped suddenly as the strong wolf spanked him again.

"Ohhh," he moaned as Sinclair worked his butt over thoroughly.

His rear had already been turning a light shade of red under his fur before his pants had come off. Now that red was beginning to show more around the edges of his panties. He whimpered. Sinclair had picked up with the intensity of the spanking where he'd left off. He hadn't gone any easier on Trevor's tender rear now that it didn't have the leather pants to protect it. He spanked hard for several minutes, making sure to cover every inch of the fox's cute rump. Then, he started all over again, only harder.

Trevor clasped his paws and held onto Sinclair's leg as the spanking got harder. The panties felt great against his tender skin, and drove him wild as they rubbed against his dripping cockhead but they provided no protection. The spanking hurt now. Each hard smack stung, but Trevor loved it. His butt felt like it was glowing, close to burning, but he still wanted more. Each impact on his tender backside sent a shock through his body that went straight to his cock. His full balls bounced back and forth as the spanking rocked his body.

Without a word, Sinclair yanked the fox's panties off. Trevor gasped as the cool air finally touched his foxhood. He felt so vulnerable, so exposed. His reddened bottom stuck up, making an easy target. He loved the feeling.

Sinclair gripped his tailbase and held his tail up. He licked his lips at the fully revealed vulpine rump. He began to spank Trevor again, hard and fast on his bare bottom. The fox cried out as the long spanking continued. Sinclair stopped for a moment and pulled the fox's legs wider apart. His cock throbbed in his jeans at the sight of the fox's full balls dangling, but he kept on working. He now spanked up and down from Trevor's tail to the middle of his thighs. The fox squirmed and whimpered on his lap at this new pain.

Suddenly, the powerful wolf began to slow down. After another minute, he ended the paw spanking with one final slap directly under Trevor's tail. The fox jerked a little as Sinclair held him like that for a moment.

"There, I think you're nicely warmed up now."

Trevor panted and sighed happily as Sinclair stroked his reddened rump.

"Now, you're ready for a real spanking," he cooed at the trembling fox.

Trevor found himself nodding enthusiastically. Being bent over a big, strong male's knee was what he had always wanted, and the hard spanking the wolf had given him with his paw had felt wonderful, but he still wanted more. He needed more, and Sinclair was going to give it to him. It scared him a little, and he didn't know how much more he could take. He hugged the wolf's leg, and realized how safe he felt now, even bent over and exposed like this.

Sinclair slowly stood up, moving Trevor to a standing position with him. He smiled at the little fox and then turned to get the bed ready.

"Why don't you look in the mirror, little fox? And see how well you're doing," Sinclair said as he gathered up the pillows in the center of the bed.

Trevor turned to look at the large mirror in the room. He quickly stripped off his t-shirt, shamelessly tossing it to the ground near where his pants were, and turned so he could see his back in the mirror. He held his breath in anticipation, and lifted his tail.

Inwardly, he sighed with satisfaction. He could see how red his skin was even through his red fur. The white fur that ran up his inner thighs and between his cheeks made it even easier to see his rosy skin in those areas.

Trevor was almost finished admiring the wolf's handiwork when Sinclair came up behind him. A flash of red caught the fox's eyes, and he looked down to see the wolf was naked now. Sinclair's long, thick cock was fully extended from his sheath.

"Hope you don't mind, I got a little more comfortable," he said with a grin.

"Now then, what have we here," Sinclair took hold of Trevor's painfully swollen and dripping foxhood.

Trevor moaned as the wolf's strong paw enveloped his maleness and began to gently stroke him.

"Looks like this naughty fox enjoyed his spanking, hmm?"

"Oh…uh," Trevor gasped, looking up at Sinclair with pleading eyes, "Yes, sir."

"Well, then," the wolf leaned down and whispered in Trevor's ear, "looks like I'm going to have to teach that naughty bottom of yours another lesson."

Trevor moaned as the wolf's breath tickled his ear, and the large, strong paw pumped his foxhood.

"Pleeeease," he moaned.

"Get on the bed, fox," Sinclair ordered, his voice like steel now.

Trevor quickly obeyed. He scurried over to the bed, past the row of spanking tools to the pillows that were piled up near the middle of the bed. Instinctively knowing what to do, he bent himself over the pillows so his reddened rump was in the air and he could lean comfortably on his arms. He opened his legs invitingly, knowing that from this angle Sinclair would be able to see his full balls along with his willing rear.

The naked wolf walked up to his side, sitting down next to him and gently stroking his back. Trevor couldn't see the row of implements now if he wanted to, and that was partially the point. He liked that, having no idea what was coming.

Soon he felt something cool and smooth against his tender backside. The cool sensation moved around his rump from cheek to cheek and under his tail, just rubbing against him. Suddenly, it was gone.

SMACK

Trevor jerked instinctively as the first strike came. Sinclair made an effort to keep him from moving too far. The wolf looked at the black leather strap in his paw. He smiled. The strap was always effective.

SMACK

SMACK

SMACK

Sinclair gave the little fox three more with the strap. Trevor had jumped a little each time, squealing just a bit. The fox loved it though. Trevor didn't know what felt better, the hard bite of the leather into his tender skin, or the stimulation to his cockhead as each time he jumped forward it was pushed into the soft pillows under him.

Sinclair worked his charge's butt over well with the strap. He wasn't keeping track, he just had the instincts for this. He stopped just as he knew Trevor had reached his limit for what he could take with the harsh leather, and then gave him one more spank with the strap beyond that. That last one made Trevor yelp and jerk forward even more. The pain seemed unbearable until his cock buried itself between the pillows, then the pleasure was overwhelming too.

Trevor whimpered and cried a bit, his whole butt felt as if it was on fire. He worried that he was reaching his limit. He didn't want this to end too soon, he wanted to show this strong wolf, whom he admired, that he could be a good little fox and take a good, long punishment.

Luckily, Sinclair knew just what he was doing. He spent a minute gently stroking Trevor's rear and telling him what a good boy he was.

Neither male was ready to stop yet.

Next, Sinclair picked up a thin, red rod made of plastic. It was about a foot long, and made a perfect little switch. He swished it through the air experimentally, and grinned at the satisfying sound it made. Trevor jumped a little at the sound, not quite knowing what to expect next.

The strong wolf held his naughty fox tightly by the base of the tail with one paw while he gently caressed Trevor's rear with the other. The fox moaned softly.

Sinclair smacked the fox's upturned rump hard with the switch. Trevor gasped and jerked forward, but was held in place by the firm paw on his tailbase. The switch had left a single red stripe across the middle of the vulpine's tender rear.

Trevor cried out each time the wolf whipped him with the switch. Each time the switch touched him, it left a blazing streak of pain across his butt. As the intensity of the spanking continued, Sinclair's tight grip on his tailbase got harder. The fox buried his head in the pillow as much as he could as the switch struck him in rapid succession. He knew he couldn't take much more, and was on the verge of begging the wolf to stop when—

"That's enough of that, I think," the wolf said to himself as he laid the vicious switch back down on the bed.

Sinclair liked to use the switch in short measures like that as no one could take it for very long. It was great for softening a fur up for more fun. Now he could tone it down a bit, and then bring the fox back up... and beyond.

"You're doing very well foxy," Sinclair softly cooed as he stroked Trevor's back. "Such a pretty fox," the wolf whispered as he began to caress the scarlet rear before him.

Next, Sinclair went for a favourite among spanking tops, but one every naughty boy dreaded... the hairbrush.

He made a couple of practice smacks in his palm, satisfied that the old brush was still a great tool. The brush had been doing this longer than he had, and who knew how many needy rear ends it had touched.

He started on Trevor's left cheek, near the top, and gradually worked his way down. Each strike was hard, and right on target. The strong wolf made each one count. Every hit overlapped the last one so some small areas got a hard smack twice in a row as he slowly worked down one cheek at a time.

The last spank to the left side was just on the fox's upper thigh. Trevor sighed a little now that Sinclair had finished that side. He then bit his trembling lip as the wolf started on his other cheek.

Trevor moaned, gripping the pillows tightly, as the long and thorough spanking continued. His cock, once a respite from the pain, was now another extension of his torture. His thick cockhead was now incredibly sensitive, as it had been gently teased by pushing into the pillows for the last half hour. It now felt over sensitive, and was still painfully hard. He needed to cum desperately, but he knew he'd better not till Sinclair told him he could. He still wanted to hold on, and show the powerful male how strong he could be too. The fox breathed a sigh of relief when the brush finally hit the top of his right thigh. Thankfully, it was over now. He knew he couldn't take much more of the brush.

SMACK

Sinclair started over from the top, this time much harder.

SMACK

Another hard and heavy blow from the hairbrush just a bit lower than last time. Sinclair continued. This time, each spank was quicker after the last one, and also closer together.

Trevor cried at the pain out loud now. The pain built upon itself as the spanking continued. All he could feel below his tail was a blazing hotness that wouldn't die down.

"I…can't—"

SMACK

"Ahhh, please I—"

SMACK

Trevor whimpered and tried to speak.

SMACK

Sinclair finished up on the left side again, before he continued, he leaned in close to Trevor. He got almost on top of the little fox, sliding his hot, dripping cock just under Trevor's tail so it rested against the tight pucker.

Trevor whimpered fearfully as felt that thick cockhead pushing against his opening. Sinclair's voice was raspy and lust-filled.

"You don't really want met to stop, do you little fox? You know you've been a naughty boy."

"Yes," Trevor timidly answered, folding his ears submissively.

"Now, I'm going to spank you harder than you've ever been spanked before," and Sinclair put his lips right against the fox's ear, "and then I'm going to fuck you just as hard."

Trevor knew he was in that time again, the time when he could stop everything and say no if he really wanted to. Past this point, no matter what he said, Sinclair wouldn't stop until they were done. He could stop now if he wanted to…if—

Sinclair pulled away and the moment passed. Trevor squeezed his eyes shut as the wolf began to harshly work his right cheek again.

SMACK

"Ah!"

SMACK

"Oh!"

SMACKSMACKSMACK

in rapid succession.

"Ah fuck!"

Sinclair held the foxtail tightly and began to smack very quickly up and down directly in the middle of Trevor's butt. He yanked up on the fox's tail, lifting his rump up a bit with it. The brush furiously attacked the tender area right under the vulpine's tail.

"Ahhh, please stop!"

Trevor almost screamed, tears streaming down his muzzle.

A shot of precum burst from Sinclair's throbbing cock as Trevor cried out. The fox was really, really good, he had to have him right now!

He tossed the brush to the side, and let go of Trevor's tail for a moment. The fox dropped back down onto the pillows, exhausted. His tail ached, his butt was on fire, but his cock was still furiously hard and dripping. He had never felt such pain before, but he loved it and found he really needed what was coming next.

The wolf gripped Trevor's tailbase and lifted it, exposing the bright red rear. He doused his cock in lube, and then tossed the bottle carelessly next to the pile of used spanking tools. Trevor parted his legs invitingly.

"Please be gentle..." he whispered.

Sinclair grinned, touching his cockhead to the tight, pink opening.

Trevor sighed, relaxing a little at the familiar feeling of a thick maleness slipping under his tail. Sinclair's fur gently teased his tender rear as he pressed against him. The wolf gripped his tail tightly in his strong paw, and thrust forward.

The fox squealed as the powerful lupine buried his member balls deep inside him. He didn't wait a second before holding the fox tightly in his arms and beginning to jackhammer his organ in and out of the stretched anus. The wolf's powerful thighs pumped hard and smacked against Trevor's reddened, tender rear. Trevor could only hold on as best he could. He'd never had it like this before, so hard and savage. The fucking was brutally animalistic. The wolf took him like he was nothing, and had no regard for his comfort or pleasure. He treated him like a toy, and Trevor loved it!

It was not long before the wolf's knot began to form. Trevor knew the feeling of having a knot lock inside him and he was prepared for it, but he didn't know that the wolf had no intention of tying with him.

The knot went in for a moment, and then quickly popped back out. It was only a little thicker than the wolf's shaft now and not nearly fully formed yet. Trevor gasped anyway as it stretched him just a little more than the wolf's thick shaft already had. The knot popped back in a few thrusts later, a bit bigger this time and stretching the fox even more.

Sinclair carefully watched his knot grow with satisfaction. It was almost ready.

His knot was about the size of a ping-pong ball now, and it took a little effort to tug it out of the fox's tight rear this time. He continued to pump his thick cock in and out of the tiny passage.

Soon, Sinclair's knot was the size of his fist and very close to full size. He popped it into the fox on one hard inward thrust. The fox quivered and moaned beneath him, and then he pulled his cock almost all the way back out. His knot tugged at the tight anus for a moment, then popped out.

The knot went in, the wolf's cock plowed deeply into Trevor's guts before the wolf dragged it back out again with another wet popping sound.

Trevor's tailhole ached from the knot's repeated entry and he was beginning to wonder when his top was going to finally tie with him now that it felt like the wolf's knot was ready.

Sinclair leaned up, gripping the fox's rear tightly, and continued his deep, hard thrusts. He continued to pop his knot in and out of the willing fox, humping him hard with it. The squeeze and sudden release on his knot as he popped it in and out of the fox felt so good, even better than just tying and cumming.

Trevor was now realizing that Sinclair was planning to breed him to the end like this. He moaned at the little pain each time the knot popped in him, stretching him wide, and tugging at his tender opening to pop back out. He began to thrust back as he got used to the feeling. He began to love it, he thought he'd loved being mounted by a thick cock, but now he loved the feeling of the softball-sized knot penetrating him over and over. His rump was still glowing from the harsh spanking, and now his tailhole ached with the fullness of Sinclair's knot pumping into him.

"Oh…yes," Sinclair gasped, the pleasure of Trevor's tailhole on his sensitive knot was now overwhelming.

Sinclair continued to thrust, his knot now fully engorged and stretching the tight fox wide.

"Here it comes foxy," the wolf gasped as he felt the surge of pleasure as cum rushed up his long shaft.

Trevor squeaked as the full knot opened him up again, bigger than ever now. He then moaned happily as he felt the flood of wolfcum filling him up. Sinclair dragged his full knot out again and quickly thrust back in, pumping another long stream of seed deep inside the fox.

The wolf filled the fox up with four more long spurts of cum. He groaned as he emptied his balls in his vulpine lover. He leaned up and breathed heavily, holding his knot gently just out-side Trevor's tailhole.

The little fox shivered with pleasure as Sinclair slowly pulled his softening member out. Trevor leaned down and sighed hap-pily, he could feel a bit of cum dripping out of his stretched tailhole. He could feel his rump still glowing warmly from the spanking fun. He suddenly gasped as he felt a strong paw slip between his legs.

"Aww, the poor foxy still needs to cum," Sinclair said as he teased Trevor's foxhood.

The wolf leaned close to Trevor again, and then nibbled on his neck for a moment, the little fox squirmed in his grasp.

"Does the good little fox want to cum?"

"Yes, sir," Trevor whimpered as Sinclair softly squeezed his member.

"Good boy," the wolf said, "then come over here."

Trevor allowed himself to be led by the paw so he was on all fours in front of Sinclair. The wolf covered his huge paw with long-lasting lube and took hold of Trevor's rampant erection. Trevor gasped as the cool, slick lube covered his cock. Sinclair gave him a little squeeze, smiling playfully. He picked up a piece of wood, the last of the spanking implements. It was slightly wider than a ruler, and very smooth. Sinclair had used it in the past, it made a good stinging spank without being as heavy as a thicker paddle.

"Now, here's what we're going to do. You're going to hump that beautiful foxcock into my paw while I spank you. I'm going to spank that butt of yours very, very hard, and I'm not going to stop until you cum."

Trevor gulped, his rear still felt very tender from earlier. He had thought that had been the hardest spanking ever, and he wasn't sure he could take much more. But, he needed to cum. He had been aroused all night, he felt like he could burst at any moment, but he needed Sinclair's help. He wanted the wolf to get him off.

"Ready?"

Trevor swallowed and nodded nervously.

"Good boy. Now raise that tail nice and high for me."

Trevor did as he was told. Sinclair smiled at him. Before another second passed, Trevor felt the sharp smack of the paddle against his exposed bottom again. He cried out, he was so tender from being spanked and then massively stretched open. Sinclair had spanked him three times with the hard paddle before he remembered he was trying to get off. He could feel the wolf grip his member, his hold slick with lube. The fox began to pump his whole length into that strong paw. The fox gasped with pleasure now as his cock finally got some attention. The pleasure after so many hours of arousal nearly made him cry with joy, just as the constant rain of spanks on his red backside made him cry with pain.

Trevor leaned forward slightly and began thrusting madly. Sinclair's paw made a tight, slick hole for Trevor's thick member to fill. He thrust deep and fast, feeling that tight grip on all eight of his inches from the thick head till his balls bounced off of Sinclair's fist. The wolf coordinated his paws very well. The one on Trevor's cock squeezed him every now and then in just the right way, while the other mercilessly paddled the fox's ass till it was blazing red again.

"Ah…oh..ahh, it hurts," Trevor whimpered as he pumped hard, desperate to cum.

"Then be a good boy and cum for me, foxy," Sinclair grinned, squeezing the foxcock a little tighter and spanking Trevor a lot harder.

"Ahhhh fu—," Trevor groaned and slowed almost to a halt as a long stream of cum blasted from his cock.

Sinclair gave him a hard smack as he slowly pushed forward, the slick paw teasing his tender cock as another huge spurt erupted from his throbbing cockhead. Trevor pulled back till the tip was inside Sinclair's paw and thrust forward again; the wolf delivered another heavy smack to Trevor's rear and the fox came again.

Sinclair put the paddle down and gathered the fox up in his arms, slowly stroking Trevor's member as he did. He held him close and pawed him the rest of the way. Trevor finished his climax held safely in the arms of the strong wolf. Sinclair held his cock gently, slowly stroking up and coaxing the last of the cum from his shaft. Trevor whimpered slightly and nuzzled into Sinclair's chestfur.

"That was…wonderful," he gasped as the wolf continued to

softly tease his member.

"Yes, you are," Sinclair replied and softly nuzzled the top of Trevor's head.

Sinclair shoved the toys off the bed and dragged them both under the covers. He quickly wrapped his arms around Trevor, holding the fox close to his chest.

Trevor's rump was sore, his tailhole still hurt from being stretched more than ever, and he felt completely happy and safe.

"Can I see you again?" Trevor timidly asked as Sinclair clicked off the light near the bed.

"Anytime," the wolf replied as he gently took Trevor's muzzle in his paw, turning the fox to face him.

And they kissed.

STUD EXERCISE PROGRAM

Trevor huffed and puffed and once again forced himself to keep going, bench-pressing another load of steel weights. He was very concerned about his image as a hot foxy, and a wolf he'd grown up with had described the perfect fox as being fit as well as being horny. So, he had decided to pump a little iron to tone up a bit.

Sinclair had snuck into the small gym that no one had really noticed before and stood surveying the scene. Trevor was working out on one of those four-sided gyms with different exercise machines on each side. At the moment he was in a lying position and working on the bench press side. The wolf decided Trevor should be exerting energy in more productive ways and decided to intervene.

Even though the room was fairly large, the air was still thick with the musky scent of a sweating, male fox. Sinclair licked his lips as the scent hit him. It didn't take much to make him hard and the fox's smell was doing it. He felt a stirring begin in his sheath as he looked Trevor up and down. The fox was so into his workout, he didn't even notice Sinclair watching him intently.

Trevor was dressed in whatever workout clothes he could scrounge together. Most of it was from a friend who had a spandex fetish. He wore a pair of tight spandex shorts that came down to mid-thigh on him. Maybe they were a little small for him because his impressive male bulge showed prominently at the front. The shorts were a lovely gay-ish purple colour, which went nicely with his tank top with "Straight Looking" written across it in pink letters. His red fur was darkened to almost maroon with his sweat and his muscles quivered with the strain.

Sinclair could stand it no longer. There was a hot fox lying there panting, grunting, and sweating and he wasn't a part of it. He strolled over and sat on the bench, straddling it and facing the yiffy foxy. He grinned down at Trevor. The fox looked a bit worried. He had a feeling his clearly-horny-as-hell wolf friend was going to disrupt his workout. He inwardly vowed not to let him succeed and that he will finish the goal he set no matter what Sinclair does to distract him.

Licking his lips and grinning, Sinclair laid his hand on Trevor's thick lump. Trevor jumped a little at the touch, but kept going. The wolf began to slowly and firmly stroke and massage the front of Trevor's spandex shorts. His paw glided easily over the smooth surface as he gave Trevor's clothed sheath a little squeeze. Despite his best efforts to ignore what was happening, Trevor's lump started to harden. Sinclair grinned wider as he felt the sheath thicken in his paw. Gripping it tightly, he leaned forward and worked his head under Trevor's shirt. The fox's scent was so thick that Sinclair could barely breathe. He loved it anyway and deeply inhaled the fox's musk. With his head still under the hot shirt, he began to lick the sweat off Trevor's furry chest. Sinclair stroked Trevor's hot sheath up and down with a slow rhythm through his tight shorts as he licked and nibbled the fox's hardened nipples. The wolf moved up a bit and nuzzled his nose along Trevor's furry underarms, one arm at a time, where his scent was strongest.

Sinclair sat up; his head was now sweaty from the heat of Trevor's body. He stripped naked and leaned over Trevor, giving the fox a good view of his hard cock sticking out of his furry sheath. Sinclair brought it down, rubbing it along Trevor's spandex shorts. He could feel the heat of Trevor's cock against his through the shorts. He looked deep into Trevor's eyes for a second before sliding his way down again. He neatly opened the fox's shorts up with one claw and pulled them from under Trevor's body. He held them up for the fox to see as he put the pre-cum stained crotch on his nose and sniffed deeply. Trevor still valiantly struggled to keep working the heavy steel stack up and down as his erect cock stuck straight out in front of him.

Without further ado, Sinclair leaned down and took Trevor's hot length into his muzzle. Trevor gasped loudly and bucked under Sinclair. His legs squirmed around trying to find some grip on the smooth floor. Sinclair worked his muzzle up and down Trevor's cock as fast as he could, pistoning up and down on the long, thick foxhood.

His muzzle began to ache from the fox's thickness, but he kept going. Every time he took the length in, he got a breath of Trevor's hot, sweaty musk as his nose rubbed into Trevor's sheath-fur. That's what kept him going every time, making him want to drive his face into Trevor's crotch while fully taking his cock. Up and down, Sinclair pumped away. Trevor's eyes watered as he tried to keep his concentration. He pushed his arms up again, they ached. He felt his balls begin to ache too. He'd been teased to ultimate hardness and badly needed a release. Trevor couldn't take it anymore, the heat, the sweat, and Sinclair's tight and hot muzzle on his maleness. Trevor's balls let go and he shot his fox-juice deep into Sinclair's muzzle.

Trevor's eyes streamed from the exertion, he pushed the stack of weights one last time in time with the last spurt of his orgasm. His body went limp and he lay there panting for several minutes as Sinclair cleaned the fox-cum off his muzzle.

"Ooh," Trevor moaned, feeling every ache. If exercising could feel this good, he would have to do it more often! He grinned up at Sinclair and asked if the big, gray wolf had an exercise program he'd like to try.

Sinclair smiled and looked to his own still-hard cock. "You can exercise me after we shower foxy."

Sinclair slipped his shorts back on and helped Trevor up from the bench. They headed off to the showers paw in paw.

Stud Exercise Program 2: Advanced Stretching

Trevor closed his locker door, tucked his fur shampoo under one arm and stepped into the shower behind him. He looked out the corner of his eye as he pulled the shower curtain aside. Sinclair was undressing a couple of lockers down. The fox whimpered as the impressive wolf slipped off his sweaty shorts, revealing his long lupine sheath. He quickly ducked into the shower as Sinclair turned around. He was a little embarrassed by how easily the wolf's simple act of undressing had aroused him.

The shower stall was quite small. The blue tiled walls were a close fit, and Trevor had just enough room to turn around. He turned under the powerful shower head, sighing as he felt the sweat being washed away and the water massaging his tired muscles. He began to slowly soap himself up. The slim vulpine had to stifle a moan as he washed his sheath. Gods, he was hard!

He closed his eyes and let the water cascade over his head. His right paw moved as if on auto-pilot as he took hold of his aching foxhood and began to stroke himself firmly up and down. He thought of what it would be like for his lover to slip in beside him and have his way with him. Between getting so caught up in his thoughts and the water blasting over his head, he didn't notice Sinclair slipping into the shower with him at first. Suddenly, he felt a paw on top of his as he stroked his foxcock. At the same time he felt the all too familiar thick sheath rubbing against his rear.

"Slow down foxy, save some of that for me," his wolf lover whispered into his ear.

"Oh, how'd you know?"

Sinclair chuckled as he nuzzled Trevor's ear. "I can always tell how bad you want it, Trevor…but it's nice to hear it anyway."

Trevor felt the wolf's paws grip his wrists tighter. Sinclair held his paws up and pressed them against the opposite wall of the shower. He held the fox immobile, his muscled body pressed hard against the fox's back. He growled into Trevor's ear as he rubbed his erect wolfhood under the fox's tail.

"So, tell me fox. Tell me how bad you need it," he growled, giving Trevor's ear a little nip.

"I need it bad, sir," Trevor whimpered, maybe a bit theatrically but he loved this kind of play.

"Good boy," Sinclair grinned and pushed forward gently, his thick cockhead rubbing against Trevor's tight little tailhole.

Sinclair braced his feet at the edges of the tiny shower stall, and then moved his paws to Trevor's shoulders. The fox kept his paws just where the wolf had left them. As he moved around, the wolf's cockhead teased gently as his partner's needy opening.

"Here it comes, sexy," the wolf whispered into Trevor's ear as he pushed forward with his muscled thighs.

"Ohhhh, ahhhh," Trevor cried out as the long, thick shaft split him open.

Sinclair didn't hold back at all. As soon as he was hilted deep inside his fox, he withdrew quickly and began to hump Trevor hard and deep. Trevor's body quivered, impaled on the shaft of thick meat under his tail. He moaned in pleasure and cried in pain at the same time. Long ago, the pain of Sinclair's rough entrance would have left him curled up in a ball, but he'd since gotten used to it and had actually begun to crave it. The pain of entry quickly faded and was replaced by a pleasant full sensation and the overwhelming pleasure of his lover's cock pummeling his prostate.

Sinclair licked and nipped at Trevor's ears as he humped hard and fast. He growled gently now and then. For his part, Trevor was so overcome with pleasure he could do little but stand there and take it. Now and then he was able to give his lover a hard squeeze on the deeper thrusts. One of these hard squeezes on his thick member made Sinclair groan deeply.

"Oh, you naughty fox," he whispered. "What am I going to do with you?"

Trevor played along, "Guess you'll have to mount me twice as hard, big boy," he growled back wantonly.

"If you insist," Sinclair gripped Trevor's neck in a mating bite and humped him harder and faster now.

Trevor was a bit taken by surprise; he hadn't thought the wolf would have been able to do him any harder than he already was. He decided to give his partner a challenge. After all, even though it was just a shower quickie was no reason it shouldn't be fun. He deftly moved his feet closer together slowly. He wondered if Sinclair even noticed at first. He gritted his teeth a little as he brought his legs together with his feet planted firmly side by side. He then leaned forward a little and squeezed his hips and buttocks together. Sinclair's thrusting had rapidly slowed by this point. Trevor moaned as the wolf's cock felt three times thicker now that he'd just made himself so much tighter.

"Damn you, fox," Sinclair grinned.

The big wolf's thrusts slowed to a crawl and he slowly thrust his aching cock deep inside Trevor's viselike passage. The fox now felt even tighter than virgins he'd been with in the past. Trevor's versatility continued to surprise him even after all the time they'd spent together. He had to give the fox a run for his money though. With a sly grin, he buried himself to the hilt inside the submissive vulpine, then reached around to tease Trevor's nipples. The fox gasped a little at the light and gentle touch on his tender nipples. Just as he was getting used to the light teasing, Sinclair squeezed them much harder. The wolf roughly pinched them between his fingertips, making Trevor whimper and press back against Sinclair's muscled body. The pain made Trevor's cock pulse with arousal, even more than it had already.

"Ready to play nice now foxy?" Sinclair asked as he continued to squeeze Trevor's tender nubs.

"Nnnn-no," the fox whimpered back, enjoying the pain and pleasure too much.

The wolf grinned, he loved it when Trevor played naughty like this. He wondered what the fox's upper limits were sometimes. He thought about how much fun it would be to find out as he squeezed Trevor's nipples even harder. He tried to control himself as that made the fox whimper and squeeze down on his wolfhood even more.

The two went back and forth three more times until Sinclair was squeezing as hard as he could for as long as he could. Trevor's nipples were swelling and turning red when he cried out and leaned forward, leaving his tailhole vulnerable once more.

"Good boy," Sinclair moved quickly. He bit down on Trevor's shoulder, holding him there.

Trevor moaned as he felt his lover's sharp teeth against his

skin. He was held hard, but completely safe. He sighed in relief and spread his legs wide, welcoming the hard mounting he so richly deserved.

Sinclair held the subjected fox close to him and hammered into his tailhole hard, fast and deep. He had been aroused for so long now, his knot was fully formed. He knew they couldn't tie here for long so he began to thrust his knot in and out of Trevor, slowly stretching the fox's body to its limits. Trevor squealed a little as the thick knot opened him up wide. Each time the knot pounded inside him, the thick wolfhood smashed against his prostate. Trevor felt his cock pulsing with need. It was torture, being so aroused and unable to touch himself because Sinclair was holding him tightly and he needed his arms to keep his balance against the shower wall.

"Oh, I'm getting close…," Trevor moaned.

Sinclair slammed forward suddenly; Trevor cried out and came hard. Sinclair slammed forward again, forcing another shot of foxcream from Trevor's abused body. Trevor felt like he couldn't take much more. Luckily, on the third hard thrust he felt Sinclair's cock unload deep inside him, filling his guts with the wolf's cum. Sinclair continued to pound away, spreading Trevor open with his thick knot, until he had emptied his balls fully. He then held himself inside the fox, keeping his knot just outside Trevor's tailhole to avoid a tie. The two stood there for another full minute, not noticing at first that the water raining down on them was turning cold.

"We should get out of here," Sinclair said as he gently nuzzled Trevor's headfur.

The fox sighed, "Do we really have to?"

Sinclair chuckled as he turned the water off. "We can get cleaned up properly at home."

When the pair came out of their shower stall, they saw that

a crowd of at least a dozen furs had gathered. All were stroking full erections.

'Were we really that loud?' Sinclair wondered to himself.

One burly bear looked lustfully at Trevor. "Hey wolf, you mind sharing that pretty vixen with the rest of us?"

Inside, Trevor gulped nervously. Outwardly, his cock throbbed to life again as he thought about it.

He was thinking about it…

NAUGHTY BOY'S LESSON

I finished getting dressed and turned to admire myself in the mirror. The white blouse and pleated skirt really completed the effect on the outside, and really made me look very girlish. What I was really proud of was underneath the skirt however; I lifted it up to see. I murred to myself as I felt my young cock stirring in my sheath. I could see the lump forming already underneath the tight, white panties I was wearing and that view made me harder still. I leaned down and caressed my legs and thighs, loving how they felt covered by the thigh-high tights. They were white also. I had been going for the Catholic schoolgirl look, and I had pulled it off quite well. I giggled to myself at how I looked, and began to slowly stroke my growing lump, moaning at how good it felt against the soft panties. A drop of precum oozed out of my tip, making a little wet spot near the frilled edge.

That's the position I was in when he came in the room. I stood perfectly still, not knowing what to do now that I had been caught. The look on his face was a picture of shock before he smiled rather evilly, turned around, and locked my bedroom door.

"Wha, what are you going to do?" I stammered.

He approached me, "I could ask you the same thing." He replied. "So, you want to be a little girl, eh?"

"Well, I just uh"

"Then, what's this?" he asked, squeezing the amble lump in the front of my panties, making my head spin with apprehension and pleasure at the same time.

"Looks like you're being a naughty little girl to me son, and I shall have to teach you a harsh lesson," he said as he pulled me by one arm over to the bed.

I was protesting all the way as he pulled my weight easily over his knee. I felt him lift my skirt next, my face flushed with embarrassment as I knew he was looking at my small, round bum in the skimpy, lacey panties. I squeezed my eyes shut when he held my bushy, red tail up out of the way, knowing what was to come now. He placed one big paw on the center of my bottom, his paw felt so huge and I, so small. He then began to spank me, hard and fast. I kicked and cried as his strong paw smacked every inch of my tender, young bottom. I had been spanked before, and it hurt every time, but never quite like this. I was still hard a rock, my pre-slickened cock slid smoothly across the material of my panties as I writhed and bucked from the hard spanking.

As I was wriggling so much, he held my tail down against my back to hold my upper body in place, and wrapped his legs against my ankles to hold them down. I was now nearly unable to move as he kept up the harsh discipline, spanking me over and over, making the skin under my fur turn as red as the fur itself.

Finally, after what felt like an hour of having my ass soundly smacked, he stopped. I cried quietly.

"Now, for your real lesson," he said, standing up.

"What?" I stammered, afraid that he intended to spank me even harder now.

He lifted me up and leaned me over the bed's edge. I heard metal, like a belt buckle behind me and began to turn my head to look.

"Keep your eyes forward boy," he roared.

I was scared stiff now, I could only lie there and not move now, hoping to avoid some of his wrath. I heard some more sounds; I wasn't sure what was happening. The next thing I felt was him lifting my skirt up again. I braced myself as I felt his paws on my pantied butt once more. This time was a little different though, he caressed my bottom and ran a finger up the cleft of my ass to under my tail. I shivered a little at this, on my tender butt this gentle touch felt very good. I braced myself again though when I felt him pull my panties down. He slipped them off completely. I thought for sure he was going to spank me with his belt this time, but I felt something different. Something hot, and hard was tickling the fur on my butt.

"You want to be a little girl, so be it. Now, I'm going to show you what it means to be Daddy's little girl."

I wondered what he meant by that, and I wondered what was now prodding under my tail. Then I realized what it was as it pressed against my tight, young hole. It was his huge cock. I had seen him in the shower once, and I knew how big he was down there. Now I shivered, knowing that it was that thick cockhead that was pressed against my tight, little hole.

"Oh please, please don't," I started to plead.

He put a calming paw on my back to hold me in place.

"Now now son, hold still. You're going to have to learn what being a little girl is all about. And what naughty little girls do is get fucked," he stated as he pushed forward suddenly.

I cried out loud as I felt him invade me.

"Oh Daddy, please don't," I squealed as his thick head forced its way past my tight ring, allowing his huge shaft to slide deeply into me.

In one long push, he planted his entire length inside me. I gasped for breath once I felt his hot, furry body pressing against mine. Precum spurted out of my still-hard cock onto the bed as he pressed me deep inside. He put his hands on my reddened bottom now to hold me in place as he began to slide his thick, long cock in and out of me. My body quivered and shook as he took me, sliding in and out faster and faster as my anus became looser. The pain eventually started to subside as I got used to his size. As he rocked my body back and forth with each deep thrust, my own cock slid back and forth on the growing patch of slick precum on the bed. I moaned as a wave of pleasure went back and forth between my full bottom and my rock hard cock.

"Yes, you moan just like a little girl too."

I sighed deeply at this, trying to ride this out till he was done taking me, but finding myself enjoying the feeling too. I felt safe, with a powerful male like Daddy in control of me.

"Oh yes, you're so tight. What a good little girl you are now," he said, almost breathless as he pounded into me.

I moaned again, my slick cock moved faster and faster along the bedsheet as he fucked me harder.

He grunted and began to slap my ass again as he pumped his maleness into me. I squealed again between pain and pleasure. Each slap made me feel him that much more, the smacks resounding off his thick, invading cock.

"You're still a very naughty little girl, I can't let you forget that," he grunted as he continued to simultaneously spank and fuck me.

"Oh yes," he said as he thrust in, "Naughty naughty little girl," he gasped as he pulled out a bit.

His rhythm increased and began to get erratic. He spanked me as hard as he pounded himself into me. I could feel him getting a little thicker now, stretching me even more. I knew he was close. I realized I was too. The warmth from my red bum spread across my body along with the feeling of fullness. It created a

wave of pleasure all over me; I could feel it in my full balls and in my painfully hard member.

Suddenly he grabbed me by the shoulders with both paws, lifting my upper body a bit as he pushed deep. I squealed once more, he was deeper than he had ever been before. He pulled out, and then went right back in, taking me fully. He pulled out and slammed hard in me one more time as I felt his hot cum splatter against my insides. I cried out, feeling him fill me up. He reached around and grabbed my throbbing cock as he thrust deep twice more, unloading his balls in me. He stroked me hard and fast as he rode the wave of his climax. This triggered my own powerful orgasm. I sprayed my load all over the bed before we both fell on it, exhausted.

We lay panting there for a moment before he pulled out. His long, softening member slide freely from my well-used tail hole. I shivered a bit as he exited me.

I rolled over to watch him stand up and begin to get dressed. "Aww, are you leaving so soon?"

"Yeah, I'm afraid so." 'Daddy' replied. "Got somewhere to be," he said as he pulled on his underwear. He looked back to me and smiled. "Same time next week, Trevor?"

I smiled back. "Of course, Daddy," I replied, giggling girlishly. That made him laugh.

I cleaned up and prepared for bed, already looking forward to another visit from my 'Daddy'.

Pulled Over

Trevor drummed his fingers on his steering wheel, tapping and singing along to one of his favourite songs on the radio. He was excited about tonight, a little "date" that Sinclair had set up for him. His wolf friend had been really sweet about encouraging his newfound confidence when it came to sex, and had begun to set him up with some more compatible furs to play with.

He adjusted himself slightly, feeling his vulpine cock grow as he thought about what tonight would hold. He'd worn what he had been told to underneath, and had worn some extremely short denim cutoffs on the top along with a belly-revealing shirt with "Vixen" embroidered on it in glitter.

"Hmm hmm hmm, hmm hmm hmm, a friend who'll tease is better," Trevor hummed along, interrupted suddenly as he heard a siren and flashing lights filled his rear-view mirror.

He pulled onto the shoulder and looked in his side mirror; he could see a hunky looking German shepherd stepping out of the car that had pulled him over.

Catch studied his clipboard as he approached the car that had been going just a bit too fast through all this construction. He looked up as he approached the bumper, taking note of the license plate again to make sure he got it down right the first time. He stopped for a moment at the bumper; he smirked a bit as he saw the FoxPride sticker.

With paws shaking slightly, Trevor unrolled his window as the officer knocked on it.

"Oooh," he said as he drank in the cop's body in his tight-fitting uniform, "Um, yes sir?"

"'Fraid you've got a broken tail light, not to mention going a bit fast back there, license and registration please."

Catch watched the fox closely as he bent over to retrieve his registration from the glove compartment. He couldn't help licking his lips slightly at the sight of the perfect vulpine rump in those tight shorts. The dog sniffed a little, his nose picking up the unmistakable scent of arousal. The fox's musk began to make his sheath throb. He tried to ignore it and stick to the matter at hand.

Soon, the fox was passing his license and registration to him. Catch looked them over closely.

"Trevor Fox, eh?"

"Yes sir," Trevor responded a little shakily, but with a slight smile.

The officer looked back and forth between Trevor and the picture on the license. He looked the fox up and down slowly; taking particular note of the bulge in the vulpine's shorts. Strangely, he thought the fox was looking at him the same way.

"I'll hold onto these a moment to check them out, why don't you pull into that alley over there so we're off the highway."

"Um...okay," Trevor started his engine again, looking over to the dark alley. He checked his rearview again, watching the cop's tight rear moving under his bushy tail. 'Murr, he's hot,' he thought to himself.

Trevor put his car into drive and headed for the alley the cop had pointed to. As he pulled into the alley, he peered out at it. He was a little nervous now; the alley was obviously old and abandoned. It looked like no one had come down here for years. All the windows on the buildings were boarded up; stray trash blew across the road. The police car pulled in behind him. Trevor noticed his lights were now off.

The hunky dog was approaching his car again.

"I need to ask you to step out of the car sir," the cop ordered.

"Okay," Trevor timidly replied.

As he got out, the police dog told him to assume the position, leaning against his car's trunk with legs parted slightly. The cop proceeded to frisk him. It wasn't as Trevor had imagined it would be. The dog's paws were strong, but gentle. The dog was almost petting him, his paws were running over his body softly. Soon he was at waist level. The dog reached around, paws gliding over Trevor's still-hard bulge, making the fox groan a little.

Catch stopped, feeling that twitching lump under his paw. He went back to it, and gave it a firm squeeze.

"What's this fox?" he asked as he squeezed down, knowing very well what it was.

"Uh, it's nothing," Trevor stammered, unable to think straight as the cop squeezed his foxhood through his shorts.

"It doesn't feel like nothing fox," Catch said, trying to sound threatening. He was enjoying watching the hot, young fox squirm. He stopped to think for a second. "I'm going to have to ask you to get undressed now."

Trevor spun around, "Huh?"

"Feels like you're carrying something there, could be a blunt instrument so I'm going to have to perform a strip search. Just co-operate and maybe I'll let you off with a warning."

"Sure," Trevor replied, smiling a little as he began to strip off his tight t-shirt, revealing his fluffy red and white chestfur.

Catch stood back to watch, a little confused. He hadn't expected the fox to comply so diligently, but he wasn't going to complain about it. The little guy was hot as hell. He secretly wondered how far he could take this.

Trevor was now unbuttoning his shorts, he wiggled from side to side, holding his thighs together as they slipped to the ground. He'd learned a bit recently about the art of provocative stripping. Then he remembered what he was wearing underneath and got a little embarrassed.

"Oh, what do we have here," Catch stepped forward to examine Trevor's undergarments more closely.

The fox was wearing a very nice pair of black, lace panties. They were thin enough that they did nothing to hide Trevor's rampant erection. Catch got closer, putting one paw midway up Trevor's shaft and squeezing firmly. The fox moaned.

"Nothing, eh," the canine muttered as he began to slowly stroke Trevor's shaft through his panties. "Looks like you're a naughty fox after all."

"Oh no sir," Trevor gasped, "I'm a good boy, honest."

"Turn around, lean on the hood," Catch grunted, his voice now choked with lust.

Trevor turned around slowly, moving up to the hood of the car and leaning forward over it. It was lower here than the trunk and he could bend over a little farther.

"Good boy," Catch said as he pulled Trevor's paws one at time behind his back.

The fox sighed a little as he felt the cool metal around his wrists, followed by the click of the cuffs being locked.

"I'm going to have to give you a body cavity search, see what else you're hiding."

"Yes, sir," Trevor moaned as he felt the officer pulling down his panties. He raised his tail invitingly.

Catch pulled a little tube of lubricating gel he kept on him for doing these kinds of searches. He used an ample amount of lube on two fingers and gently parted the fox's gorgeous rump cheeks with one paw. His doggie cock throbbed in his tight uniform pants as he saw the vulpine's tight, pink pucker. He placed his lubed fingertips against Trevor's opening, the coolness of the lube made the fox gasp a bit, then Catch thrust both fingers in hard.

"Awww, god," Trevor cried out at the sudden intrusion. Despite the sudden pain of entry, his cock sprung to full attention.

Trevor looked over to the Shepherd's paw on his shoulder. He had big paws, with thick masculine fingers. Trevor quivered happily, feeling fingers moving inside him, and he knew that at least two of those thick fingers were now deep under his tail.

Catch drove his fingers in deeper, spreading them apart inside the fox's tight ass. He felt the lump of Trevor's prostate and massaged it with his fingertips, which made the fox moan wantonly. He pushed his fingers in as deep as possible; the fox's tailhole seemed to swallow them up. That's when Catch knew the fox really wanted this, and he didn't hold back anymore. He pulled his fingers out, leaving the fox gasping. Catch examined Trevor's tailhole, and saw it was puckering slightly, almost begging to be filled again.

"I need to do a deeper inquiry," he said as he unclipped his baton from his belt.

"Ooh, yes sir," Trevor moaned lustfully, almost sluttily.

Catch ran his black baton up the insides of Trevor's bare legs. He ran the smooth tip over the fox's dangling white-furred balls. With a wicked little grin, he gave the vulpine's balls a little tap with the baton. Trevor moaned at the sudden sensation on his balls, he could feel his cock shoot out a long stream of precum as his balls were gently tapped. Catch trailed the baton's smooth, black tip up along Trevor's sack, letting his balls dangle again, and slowly began to press the rounded end between the fox's cheeks.

Trevor suddenly felt something different than what he'd been expecting, something thick and rounded was pressing insistently against his tailhole. He realized that it was the foot-long thick baton that had been swinging from the police dog's belt. It was so big looking, he'd never taken anything like it before.

"Wait, I don't know if I can-Ahhh," Trevor cried out as Catch started shoving forward, the two inch thick end of the baton slowly began to spread him open wide.

Catch pushed down on Trevor's back as he continued to jam his baton up the fox's rear. The vulpine's tailhole had opened up nicely after a moment, allowing the baton's length to start invading his depths. Trevor was still crying as the thick tip continued to spread him apart on the inside. Soon, Catch had shoved about eight inches of the blunt object inside his captive.

Trevor cried out, his paws straining at the cuffs around his wrists. He squirmed on the hood of the car as he was deeply invaded. He felt his thick, foxhood bumping against the metal of the car, and knew he was painting it with his precum. He was still raging hard, and despite the pain he knew he wanted more. His back arched slightly, tail raising high, as he pushed himself back a little, feeling the baton's thick shaft pushing slightly at his insides.

"More foxy?" Catch asked, a little amazed at Trevor's endurance.

"Yes...Sir!" Trevor gasped, begging for it with tears streaming down his muzzle.

Catch smiled and dragged the baton out till just the tip remained to hold the fox's wanton hole open.

"Here it comes boy," Catch stated, matter-of-factly as he began to smoothly thrust the baton's length back into his squirming prisoner.

Trevor cried and moaned simultaneously as the thick club was pounded into him. Catch was now pumping it hard and fast, the black shaft now slick with lubricant and fox sweat. The police dog slowly increased how much of the shaft he thrust into the willing fox, pushing an inch more at a time, going deeper and deeper under the fox's tail. Catch looked down and noticed

Trevor's balls were pulled up tight to his body as he thrust the tenth inch in. He wondered if Trevor could possibly cum from this when Trevor suddenly cried out.

"Oh yes, more, harder. Oh gods, pull my tail sir," Trevor practically ordered the police dog, who now felt as if he'd gotten into more than he'd bargained for, not that he wasn't enjoying himself of course.

He took hold of the base of Trevor's tail with his free paw,

squeezing it tightly in a powerful grasp. He tugged up hard and sudden as he pumped another inch deeper, opening Trevor up deeper than he'd ever been taken before.

"Ahhhh, yes harder sir mmm harder," Trevor squealed and shivered, his cock pulsing with need. Trevor desperately need to cum now, feeling more and more on the edge of a huge orgasm with every inch the canine shoved into him, his cock demanded attention as it throbbed almost painfully. Trevor whined, unable to touch himself with his cuffed paws.

Catch smiled, watching Trevor's tight balls and raging cock. The fox was extremely well-hung for a little fur. He wanted to see if he could make the fox cum just by pounding his sexy rear and if he couldn't he could at least keep him on the edge for a good long time. He pistoned the thick club in and out, back and forth, faster and faster as he pushed Trevor closer to the edge.

Trevor could feel it coming now, the familiar pressure building up inside him as he was spread open and his prostate was assaulted by the heavy pounding he was receiving. He bucked backwards, pushing himself farther down, humping himself back harder and faster. He moaned long and loud as his foxhood tensed up, his whole body quivered with ecstasy, and his full balls released their load. Long hot streams of foxcum shot up the length of his shaft, splattering all over the side of the car and on the ground. Just as his powerful orgasm was starting to wind down, the police dog reached around and grabbed his long, thick cock. The dog gave him a hard squeeze, squeezing up from the base all the way along his shaft. Trevor moaned as more cum was forced from his body, and he shook in pleasure as the dog teased him. He collapsed forward against his car, his muscles like jelly, and he was unable even to squeeze the thick invader from his tailhole.

Catch stood back, admiring his vulpine captive. The fox was

shaking and covered in sweat, his cock dripping obscenely and his beautiful rear still impaled on his police baton. He realized then that he was still hard as a rock himself when his cock reminded him with a painful throb. He quickly unzipped his pants and released his canine maleness. His cock had already extended all the way out of his sheath, and his knot was already half formed. He grabbed the limp fox by the back of the neck and pulled him down off the car.

"On your knees, fox," he ordered.

Trevor yelped slightly as the baton struck the ground and sent a sharp shiver through his oversensitive body. Catch leaned over and positioned the baton so it was firmly and deeply lodged inside the fox again.

"That's it boy, you keep that in there good and tight."

"Yes, sir," Trevor sighed weakly.

He was tired from an extremely powerful climax, but was happy the night was not quite over yet. The dog grabbed his headfur and turned his muzzle. He opened wide as the hunky Shepherd fed his hard dogcock to him.

Catch sighed as he felt the fox's warm muzzle around his cock. He was amazed at how willing this young vulpine was to please him. Trevor was now eagerly sucking and licking along the underside of his shaft. He began to slowly hump in and out of the hot, tight muzzle around him, feeling his need beginning to build already. Catch knew he couldn't make this last very long, he almost felt like he would cum any second. Then he felt Trevor's muzzle open wide and his lips gripped his engorged knot and squeezed down hard, imitating a tie. Catch grunted; the fox knew exactly how to get him to shoot. He moaned and futilely tried to hold back and make the pleasure last longer, but soon he was pumping hard and fast, feeling himself getting closer and closer. A few seconds later, and he half howled/half whimpered and filled Trevor's willing muzzle with his canine seed. The police dog stood and panted for several moments, trying to regain his ability to move as Trevor gently sucked and licked his remaining cum from his sensitive cockhead. He reluctantly pulled himself out of that wonderful warm, sucking muzzle and began to tuck himself back into the pants of his uniform.

"Good…fox," he panted, "I'll let you off with a warning after all."

Catch staggered back, his legs now very shaky. His mind raced back through the events and he could scarcely believe he had done this. Now the little fox was looking up at him expectantly, licking cum from his lips.

"Um…yeah?" Catch asked, a little uncertainly.

"Well, if you're all done, then uncuff me silly," Trevor giggled a little.

Catch blinked twice before realizing what he should do. He leaned down next to Trevor, and released the fox's bound paws. Trevor then stumbled to his feet as Catch made to walk away.

"Excuse me officer, can you help me with something?"

The once-intimidating police dog turned around, "Yeah?" he asked.

Trevor once again bent over the hood of his car and raised his tail.

"This," he said, pointing to the foot long black baton still firmly lodged under his bushy tail.

"Oh sorry," Catch couldn't believe he'd forgotten his baton.

He put one paw gently on Trevor's rump, and took the end of the baton in the other.

"Ready?"

"Yeah, just take it out slow."

Catch began the slow process of easing the baton back out. Trevor groaned long and loud as it was pulled out. He felt it pulling out of his body inch by inch, leaving a feeling of emptiness behind that he'd not felt since the first time he'd been mounted. After what felt like half an hour, but was really only a few minutes, Trevor's tail drooped down, covering his now empty rear.

"Ooh, thank you sir."

"Um, sure," Catch was able to get out before quickly retreating to his police car.

Trevor briefly wondered why he seemed so flustered. Then realized he was standing naked down a dark alley. He quickly gathered up his clothes, tugged his shorts on and made his way home. As he pulled out of the alley, it started to rain.

Catch radioed base and informed them he was going off duty early due to illness. He went home and pawed off, thinking of the sexy young fox he'd just dominated. He'd thought he might get a little show at most, but Trevor had been a lot more willing than he'd have expected in his wildest dreams. He was defiantly going to be on the lookout for more foxes with broken taillights from now on.

Epilogue 1:

Sinclair's phone rang.

"Yeah?"

"Hey hon," Trevor's unmistakable bubbly voice came over the line.

"Hey yerself, how'd tonight go?"

"Oh, just wanted to let you know it was wonderful. The fur you hooked me up with really got into the part. Anyway, letting you know I'm home safe and sound now."

"That's great Trev. You can tell me all about it this weekend. Still coming over, right?"

Trevor's voice was half-chocked with a yawn, "Uh-huh, I'll call you later in the week. I'm going to bed now though. Sleepy foxy."

The wolf chuckled, "Sweet dreams, you naughty fox."

Epilogue 2:

Across town a rain-soaked collie in a very fake looking cop costume was standing in a phone booth. His paws shivered as he dialed.

Sinclair's phone rang...again.

"Yep?"

"Hey man, your fox friend didn't show."

"Huh?"

"Yeah man, I rented this costume and waited on the expressway just like you said, but he never showed up."

Sinclair was so confused he actually scratched his head as he thought, and then the operator said "Seven cents more for the next three minutes".

"I'm outta time man, I gotta go. Next time you set me up with someone lets make sure it's somewhere warm. Laters," the collie hung up and pulled his costume uniform shirt closer to him.

Sinclair looked at the phone as if it were an alien artifact for a moment before hanging it up and going to bed.

Compressions and Rarefactions

1. Trevor and Sinclair

Sinclair woke up to a sensation he didn't recognize. The fur around his tail felt wet and something hard was poking under it. He looked down and saw Trevor's blackfurred paws twitching as they wrapped around his waist, and he realized his vulpine friend was trying to hump him.

"Trevor, what're you doing?"

"Yiff yiff yiff," Trevor panted to himself.

Sinclair realized what was going on, the foxy was having a wet dream which was about to get really wet. He deftly reached behind him and gripped the hard foxy cock in one paw, beginning immediately to pump it up and down. He flipped around to get a better angle, never breaking his rhythm. Trevor was quivering now, lying flat on his back and thrusting wildly into Sinclair's tight paw.

"That's it, cum like a good foxy," Sinclair whispered into the smaller fur's ear.

The increased stimulation of Sinclair's squeezing paw and the impending orgasm began to wake Trevor up.

"Oh…what's?" Trevor gasped, his body already tensing up to release. He turned his muzzle, breathless and still bleary eyed from sleep. Sinclair leaned down and kissed him deeply, still rapidly stroking the pulsing foxcock.

"Mrrf," Trevor protested for a moment, still not sure what was going on, and then he moaned into the kiss, his cries stifled by Sinclair's muzzle as he came. A clear jet of foxcum, quite unlike his usual fire hose of seed shot straight up, landing in a sticky stream on his belly.

Sinclair broke the kiss, looking down at Trevor, who gasped and blinked his eyes rapidly to get rid of the sleep in them.

"Ooh, what just happened?"

The big wolf smiled as he continued to slowly stroke up Trevor's length, squeezing a few more drops out.

"You were sleepyiffing, silly foxy."

"Really? It didn't feel like it usually does when I cum."

Sinclair laughed, "Haven't you ever had a wet dream before?"

Trevor looked a little embarrassed, and Sinclair knew right away that this had been his first. He decided to change the topic slightly.

"So, who were you dreaming about?"

"Huh…oh, let me think. I was dreaming I was having sex with you."

"Heh, cool."

"Actually, I was mounting you."

"Really?" Sinclair gently scratched the fox's chestfur. "That's funny."

Sinclair rolled out of bed to use the bathroom. As he did, Trevor sat up.

"Why's that funny?"

"Huh?" Sinclair called back as he looked around the countertop for his toothbrush.

Trevor crawled on all fours on the bed towards him.

"Why is me topping you funny?"

Sinclair laughed, "You're a fox silly." He ruffled Trevor's head-fur then went to have a shower.

Trevor sat back down on his haunches, he hugged his tail to his chest and nibbled on the tip as he thought about that.

Half an hour later they were in the kitchen. Trevor was sitting, thinking with his head leaning in his paws, as Sinclair prepared breakfast.

"Did having a wet dream really unnerve you or something?" he asked while mixing an omelet.

"Why do you ask?"

"No reason, except you seem to be very quiet this morning. Usually you're a ball of energy and I can't keep up before my third cup of coffee."

"Okay, I'll tell you if you promise not to laugh."

Sinclair turned around, leaning on the countertop with a quizzical look on his muzzle.

"Okay, I'll bite. I promise not to laugh," he said in as serious a tone as he could muster first thing in the morning.

Trevor sat up straight in his chair, looked the imposing wolf right in the eye and defiantly stated.

"I want to top."

Sinclair held true to his word, he didn't laugh. He put down the towel he'd been using to dry his paws and approached Trevor slowly. He leaned down, looking down into the fox's pretty green eyes.

"Aren't you happy being a bottom?" he asked gently as he leaned in to nibble at Trevor's neck.

"Oooh," Trevor moaned as Sinclair nibbled and gently bit at his neckfur, turning him into a submissive puddle.

"I love being a bottom," he sighed, whimpering and biting

his lower lip as one of Sinclair's paws gripped his rapidly filling sheath.

Trevor's lupine lover picked him up and laid him on his back on the kitchen table, his tail hung over the edge. Sinclair deftly tossed his only item of apparel, his "Yiff the Cook" apron, onto the chair Trevor had been sitting in.

Trevor looked back at his lover as he prepared. Sinclair lifted Trevor's feet and placed them on his shoulders. Trevor grinned and looked down to see Sinclair's cock was raging hard, and his own foxhood was getting hard again also.

"Wait," he blurted out just as the wolf was about to press his thick cockhead to his tailhole. "I'm serious," he paused for a moment to choose his words. "I love being a bottom, but I want to try topping too."

"You have," Sinclair replied with a grin. "You topped Ray."

Trevor's ears lowered a little as he replied, "Yeah, but you had him first. I want someone to...I dunno, dominate by myself."

Sinclair smiled. "Okay, I'll find you someone to mount."

"Really?" Trevor's face lit up.

"Really," Sinclair stated and thrust forward.

"Aww gods," Trevor gasped, his back arching as Sinclair's long, thick wolfhood spread him open.

Trevor couldn't think anymore now that the huge wolf was pounding his tail once more, and that familiar sting of being split open was rapidly replaced with the full feeling and overwhelming pleasure of being soundly penetrated. His body was on fire with sensation; he closed his eyes and nibbled on one fingertip as Sinclair's paws roamed his chest, tweaking his nipples and deeply scritching his chestfur.

"So, who're you...uh, gonna hook me up with," Trevor grunted out, trying to keep up with Sinclair's ability to talk and screw at the same time.

"There's only one natural submissive for a fox like you," Sinclair responded, putting his hands on Trevor's shoulders and thrusting harder.

Trevor's legs went like jelly under the hard pounding; they spread wide as the wolf's powerful hips thumped against his up-turned rear.

"Who…would…oh god…that be?"

"A," Sinclair grunted as his knot swelled up and began to pop in and out of Trevor's rear, "bunny."

"Oh yeah, tie with me," Trevor panted, "Why's that?"

"Well," Sinclair grunted and thrust forward hard, burying his knot deep in Trevor's tail. "They have easy access tailholes."

Trevor giggled at little at that before moaning deeply again as his wolf lover pounded him hard and fast now, the thick knot pulling at his opening from the inside. Sinclair leaned forward now, pushing himself off the floor and pumping as hard as he could, feeling himself getting closer and closer. The pair didn't speak anymore as they both concentrated hard on the sensations of their bodies. The big wolf gasped as he finally felt his cum shoot into his fox's warm body, releasing the pressure in his balls and cock. Trevor sighed happily as he felt the familiar warm flood filling him up. He reached up and caressed his partner's muzzle as he was filled. A moment later and he too moaned and whimpered as the wolfcock's insistent prodding on his prostate pushed him over the edge, making his cock cover his white, fluffy chest in foxcream.

Sinclair held still for a moment to recover, and then leaned down to kiss the fox full on the muzzle. The two kissed for a long moment before Sinclair stood up again, still locked inside Trevor for now. Then the wolf leaned over and picked up the cordless phone that was lying on the table, just behind Trevor's head.

"I'll go ahead and give the bunny a call, get you all set up," he said as he was pushing buttons

"Okay, cool," Trevor responded as he flexed his tailhole on the thick knot holding him open. "What's his name by the way?"

Sinclair got a slightly puzzled look on his face for a moment. "Y'know, I never stopped to ask. I've just always referred to him as the bunny. Heh."

Trevor chuckled, "I'll find out for you."

2. Sinclair and Darkie

After having seen Trevor off for the night, Sinclair cleaned up the kitchen from this morning's fun. There was milk everywhere. All kinds: wolf, fox and the more traditional 2%. That thought made him smile as he tossed his dishrag into the hamper for later. He'd never thought he'd ever become the domestic type, but he managed to keep the place pretty tidy normally. The wolf puttered around his apartment for a few more minutes before he realized it was getting late, almost club time. He figured by the time he was done showering and dressing, it'd be time to go. It wouldn't do to arrive at The Raven too early. By the time he showed up, there would be enough of a crowd to make it worthwhile. He was really in the mood to spend time with Trevor, but he knew Bunny would keep him busy for most of the night. The wolf would have to find another sub for the night. He smiled a bit; it would be fun to go "hunting" again.

"Hey pup, you lookin' for a good time?"

Sinclair inwardly groaned as he put his drink down on the bar. "You know I don't play with bears, Bruno," he replied without turning.

"Yeah, I know," the hirsute ursine said as he hopped up on the stool next to Sinclair.

"So, why'd you ask if you already know the answer," the wolf grinned back as his fellow dom.

"Well, you know I love lupines, but it's so hard to find a willing playmate. You're all so…," he paused, clicking his tongue as he thought of an appropriate word, "predatory."

Sinclair chuckled. "That, we are," he agreed as he sipped his rum and coke, hold the rum.

"I figured, since you know most of the wolves around here, you could point me in the right direction."

"Hmm, okay then," Sinclair turned, leaning his back against the bar as he scanned the crowd.

The wolf's keen eyes scanned over the bodies writhing against each other on the dance floor. He then strained his nose, sniffing out a likely body. He picked one out quickly, a familiar scent. Submissive wolves were indeed hard to find for non-wolves. For a wolf, all you had to do was find a wolf less dominant than you. Prove yourself more dominant and you had a willing partner for the night. Problem was, very few wolves were willing to subjugate themselves to another species. Sadly, there was a kind of stigma around true submissives in wolf society.

"Found one."

"Show me," Bruno leaned in close as Sinclair tried to find with his eyes what his nose had already told him.

"Shit, he's caught already," Sinclair chuckled as he saw what had happened. "By a fox no less."

"Dammit, guess I'll have to settle for that flirty cat instead," the ursine growled as he followed Sinclair's look. They smiled as they watched a submissive wolf, collared and leashed, being led out of the Raven by his new master for the night.

"Have fun with that cat, Bruno," Sinclair said as the bear walked off, slightly disappointed.

"At least he'll still get laid tonight, hmm."

"Yeah, that's true," Sinclair turned again to see who had spoken.

"So, how about it big boy, are you looking for a good time," the female cheetah asked him.

Sinclair laughed quietly at his old friend, "Celina, you know you're not my type love."

"I know baby," she purred and rubbed against him, "pussy just isn't what you're used to, is it?"

"Not at all," he grinned back, reaching around to give her a quick grope, stopping when he heard a small whimper in the darkness. "Who do you have with you, my dear?"

"Oh, this old thing," she replied, tugging on a leash.

Sinclair could now see a nearly naked black panther was crouched just behind Celina, he moved closer as the metal chain tugged on his collar.

"This, my dear wolf is the pussy I was referring to."

"I see, your new pet I take it."

"Quite, but I'm afraid I'm having some problems with him."

"Hmm," Sinclair grinned, playing along with whatever scene Celina had with her pet panther. "Such as?"

"There are some lessons he needs to learn that I could use some help with teaching him. If you're interested, of course."

"Why, you know I'm always willing to help. Now, tell me all about it. Has he been a naughty boy?" Sinclair felt his sheath stir in his tight pants. "Do you need me to put him over my knee for you?"

"Heh," the slim cheetah laughed, "Not at all. He's quite obedient, and even if he weren't I'm fully capable of making that delicious rear quite red."

"Of course, of course. So, what lesson would you have me teach your pet?"

"Oh, it's terrible dear wolf. Darkie tries so hard to please me, but he's so very small you see. His little cock just doesn't satisfy me at all."

With that, the panther whimpered, turning away slightly and lowering his ears in shame.

"Oh my, terrible. Such a big kitty too."

"I know, I know. He's quite tall when I allow him to stand, but the most important part of him is so tiny. What I need you to do, old friend, is show my little panther what a real fucking feels like," Celina licked her lips and grinned.

Sinclair was beginning to really like the sound of this. "Tell me Celina, has he ever been taken?"

"No," she smiled. "He's never been with a male before. He thinks he might be straight."

At this, they both laughed while Darkie whimpered and looked to the floor. He saw out of the corner of his eye as his mistress passed the end of his leash to the imposing male wolf.

"Oh, take this too please," Celina passed a digital video camera to Sinclair. "I want to see him squeal, okay?"

"Consider it done," Sinclair licked his lips and gave the leash a tug, "Come boy, tonight you belong to me."

"Yes...master," the panther sighed, trotting after the wolf as they left the club. Behind him, his mistress told Sinclair to be sure and mark him as she continued laughing.

**

Sinclair pulled his new plaything into the bedroom of his apartment by his leash.

"Now boy, you wait right there."

The wolf left the panther alone, closing the door behind him. He knew being left alone, not knowing what to expect, enhanced the fear and anticipation of what might happen. He hadn't wanted to ask too many questions at the club in an attempt to keep up the scene they'd been created on the fly, but he did need some answers. He quickly dialed Celina's cell, she picked up on the first ring.

"You got home fast, couldn't wait to try him out, eh?" She chuckled.

"You've got me figured out, don't ya."

"Okay, here are the details."

Now armed with his submissive's likes, dislikes and safeword, Sinclair was ready. He entered the bed room and set up a tripod in the corner. He placed the camera Celina had given him on it and zoomed in on the center of the bed. The panther watched him quietly as he set up the video camera. He walked up to the slim panther, who was crouched on the floor of the bedroom.

"Okay boy, first you have to get a look at what you'll be taking tonight," he smiled down at Darkie. "Take out my cock," he ordered.

Darkie swallowed and sat up on his knees. He slowly moved his paws, which were shaking slightly, to Sinclair's belt. He began to open it up slowly.

"Faster boy, I don't have all night here," the wolf commanded, sounded slightly aggravated.

The panther moved faster, quickly opening up the wolf's top button and unzipping him. He whimpered as he saw his new master's plump sheath for the first time.

"Yes pet, you'll take every inch by the end of the night."

Sinclair finished getting undressed, carelessly tossing his clothes on the floor. He stood naked in front of the nervous feline.

"Strip and follow me," he said simply as he turned towards the bathroom.

Darkie did as he was told, throwing his own clothes into a pile next to the wolf's. He followed Sinclair to the master bathroom. The wolf ushered his new pet in before him as he plucked the camera off its tripod.

"I drank too much tonight," he told the panther. "I've really got to go now. Get on your knees, next to the toilet there."

Darkie obeyed, crouching down next to the commode.

"Lean your head over the bowl."

The panther sighed, his ears flat against his head as he bent over, knowing what was to come. Above him, his master pulled down his sheath to let his large, but still flaccid, wolfcock hang out.

Once Darkie was in position, Sinclair grinned and turned on the camera.

"Here we go," he said as the show began.

Sinclair sighed as he relieved himself. He looked down at the panther as his warm urine sprayed the feline's shoulders and arms. He carefully aimed higher up, soaking his neck and moving up to his closed muzzle. The wolf covered his pet's face, letting it soak in and making the panther's black fur that much darker.

"Open up, boy," the wolf commanded, in his most imposing voice.

Darkie squeezed his eyes shut tight and opened his muzzle, gulping a little as the hot wolf piss splashed onto his tongue and down his throat. The torrent seemed to last forever, but in reality was only a few seconds and Sinclair had moved the stream farther down. He carefully marked the panther as his, coving the subjugated animal from head to toe.

Sinclair held back a little, holding some in.

"Now, look at me and spread your legs. Let's see that little cock of yours."

Darkie moaned, feeling his face burning with shame as he opened his eyes and slowly turned, parting his legs to reveal all of his body to his new owner.

The panther mewed a little as the wolf laughed at him. "Your mistress was right, boy. You could never please a woman with that pathetic little thing."

Sinclair released another stream, this time directly on the

panther's crotch. Darkie moaned as the wolf's warm piss covered his rock-hard erection and flowed down over his dangling, black balls. His feline member stood up from his body, its full length of just under five inches displayed for his master's amusement. Gradually, the stream of urine trailed off as Sinclair finished marking him.

"Ah, much better. So far, you're good for pissing on, boy. Let's see if I can teach you some other tricks, eh."

Sinclair reached down and grabbed the panther by the scruff of his neck, pulling him along like an errant kitten. The panther hung limply like a rag doll from his paw as he stopped to quickly remount the camera and make sure it was again aimed towards the bed. He then dragged his pet over to the bed, pulling the panther on after him. He sat up on his knees, the panther as lying down in front of him.

"Now," he grabbed Darkie's headfur and pulled him close, rubbing his now fully hard wolfcock against the panther's muzzle. "Give it a good lick, little panther."

The panther tentatively began to lick along the length of Sinclair's hard shaft.

"Ooh, that's it boy," the wolf moaned, the panther's small rough tongue felt very good on the tender flesh of his wolfhood.

Sinclair was raging hard now. He hadn't played with a sub in this way in a long time. He was surprised at how much it had turned him on. He looked down. Darkie was now licking him all over, nuzzling gently at his thick knot. Sinclair took hold of his shaft and slowly guided his dripping cockhead to his pet's muzzle.

"Now, lick up my cum, then take my cock into your muzzle."

Darkie complied, quicker than Sinclair had expected for a formerly straight fur. The feline's rough tongue on his tender cocktip sent a shiver through his body as Darkie lapped up his precum. Soon, his painfully throbbing cockhead had disappeared between the black panther's lips.

"Oh yeah, that's it. Good boy," Sinclair moaned as he began to slowly hump the panther's muzzle.

"You're an excellent cocksucker. Hmm, I bet you're not really straight, are you? You suck dick way too well, my boy."

Darkie blushed under his fur and squeezed his eyes shut. He felt so ashamed sucking this big male's cock like this and feeling, deep inside, how much he enjoyed it. He didn't want to admit that he loved it, and longed to feel this thick member under his tail. He moaned as he thought about what it might feel like, hoping he might find out tonight.

"Good boy, ooh," Sinclair gently caressed the panther's cheek as he complimented him. "Mmm, I bet you've gone down on lots of males. You suck as well as any hustler."

The shamed panther blushed hard again as he took more of the wolf's shaft in his muzzle, sucking hard and moving his rough feline tongue up and down the underside of his master's member.

"Oh, now slow down boy," Sinclair slowly pulled his cock away from the panther's eagerly sucking muzzle. "You've gotten me nice and hard. I can honestly say, you're the best little cocksucker I've ever encountered. However, you know where a cock like this really belongs, don't you boy?"

Darkie whimpered fearfully. "Yes, sir," he replied.

"Well, why don't you tell me boy. Where do you want me to put his?" Sinclair asked as he gripped his shaft, squeezing gently as precum oozed from his thick tip.

"Under my tail, sir," Darkie whispered.

"I couldn't hear you, boy," Sinclair roared. "Tell me what you want me to do."

"I uh…I," the panther stammered.

"Tell me you want me to fuck you like the little cockslut you are."

"I…I want you to fuck me, sir."

"And how do you want me to fuck you, boy?"

"Hard sir, please," Darkie sighed, defeated. He looked away, his voice cracking. "Please fuck me hard, sir."

Sinclair reached forward, grabbing Darkie's chin. He turned the panther's head so they looked into each other's eyes.

"I will," he told him in no uncertain terms. "I will fuck you all night, till you squeal like a kitten."

The wolf released his pet and sat up. "Now, get my cock nice and wet. I was going to go easy on you your first time, but you've proven yourself such a good little cockslut, I know you don't need the lube I had for you."

"Th-thank you, sir," Darkie almost cried as he leaned over to get the wolf's long, thick member ready to take him.

The wolf smiled and gently gripped the panther's headfur as he felt the feline's rough tongue bathing his cock again.

"Mmm, that's very good kitty. Get it nice and slick for your tight tailhole."

Sinclair let his pet slurp at his cock a few more minutes before he was ready.

"That's enough pet, that should be wet enough for your obviously experienced ass."

"Yes, sir," Darkie pulled off the lupine meat slowly, saliva trailing from his muzzle.

"Now, turn around for me and raise your tail. Show me your cockhungry tailhole."

The submissive panther slowly turned around, his paws quivered gently as he gripped the pillow his master had put there for him. He was scared. His mistress had teased his tailhole with toys before and even made him wear a buttplug while he plea-

102

sured her orally, but he'd never taken a real male or anything as big as his master's cock before. He was afraid, but also excited. His own small cathood throbbed eagerly, dripping precum down his short shaft. 'Oh gods, please be gentle,' he silently begged just before he felt his master's thick cockhead slipping under his raised tail.

Sinclair moved into position behind his pet. He gasped a little as the panther's soft fur brushed past his sensitive tip. He couldn't believe how turned on he was. Soon, he felt his pet's warm pucker against him and he knew he was ready.

"Here it comes, boy," Sinclair grunted as he pushed forward slowly.

Darkie gritted his teeth as he felt the pressure building under his tail, he tried to force his body to relax and let the thick wolfhood in but he was just too tight. He felt his master give a slightly harder push and with a grunt, the wolf was in him. He mewled loudly as his master's enormous cockhead forced open his almost-virgin tailhole. Once the head opened him up wide, the long shaft followed easily, sliding deep inside him. He was grateful that his master was just holding in him for now, his wolfhood nestled deep inside.

Sinclair groaned, breathing heavily as he slipped in all the way to the knot. 'Holy shit, he's tight. This really is his first time,' the wolf thought to himself in amazement. He'd thought Celina had been teasing him a bit just to play along with the scene. 'Well, he seems to be enjoying himself anyway,' he chuckled to himself and decided to just enjoy himself till his pet used a safeword.

The wolf began to slowly pull out of his pet. Inch after thick inch slid out of the panther's tight hole, making the feline quiver.

"Oh, ahhh," the submissive panther whimpered. "Oh gods!" he yelped as his master once again hilted himself deep inside.

With only his own spit for lubrication, this was a rough

mounting. He bit down and bore out the pain as the thick wolf-cock split him open again and again, pumping deeper and deeper inside his once-virgin hole with each inward thrust. Soon, the pain dissipated and was replaced with extraordinary pleasure as his master's maleness pumped harder and faster, pressing his insides in all the right places.

Sinclair heard his pet begin to pant, making little gasps of pleasure with each deep thrust. He was happy to see the panther enjoying himself.

"Good boy, you like this don't you."

"Oh oh oh, yes sir," the feline panted back, barely able to speak.

"I knew a little slut like you could handle my cock easily. Guess I don't need to worry about going easy on you, eh."

Darkie whined fearfully, the rough mounting felt good now but he was still scared of his master's size. The wolf was so big, huge compared to his own little cathood. He wanted to please his new master, he wanted to be a good boy and make his mistress proud.

Suddenly, he felt the full weight of his master on his back. The strong wolf was holding him down with his body weight now, still pumping deeply into him. The panther's master pinned him down, pressed flush against the bed as he mounted him savagely now.

"Oh, ahhh," Darkie buried his face in the pillow as his master took him hard, fast and deep. "Ohh, please master…I can't take it…I"

"Yes you can," Sinclair cut off the panther's protests. "You can take all of me, every" he thrust hard inward, drawing out slowly, "last," he thrust in hard again, this time his swelling knot popped inside for a second before he withdrew once more, "inch!" With that, Sinclair thrust forward harder than before; his engorged knot was forced against the panther's needy tailhole before making a loud pop as it was forced inside hard.

"Ahhh, master! You're too big, it hurts," the panther screamed, crying into the pillow.

Sinclair continued to thrust his trapped cock into his pet, his thick knot pulled hard at the insides of the panther's desperately clenching tailhole. He wrapped his arms around his pet's chest, holding him close as he leaned down and took the scruff of the panther's neck in his powerful jaws. He took the panther's neck scruff in a mating bite as he continued to pump his tailhole hard and fast.

The panther's body shivered and shook in pleasure as the big wolf dominated him utterly and used him like a toy for his pleasure. This was what he wanted, this was what he needed. He felt the bite on his neck intensify as his master's body went rigid for a moment. The wolf sighed deeply. A moment later, the panther closed his eyes in bliss as he felt the warm flood of cum filling him up. The hard mounting continued on for several more hard thrusts as his master emptied his load of lupine seed deep inside his needy tailhole. He felt the pressure on his insides as the wolf filled him up.

"Thank you master," he whispered gently as the wolf slowed to a halt, then began to gently lick his neck.

Sinclair panted softly while lapping at the bite wound he'd left on his pet's scruff. He was exhausted now, he'd cum incredibly hard but the game wasn't over yet.

The pet felt his master lifting him up. He moaned as the thick cock inside him changed position, pressing hard against his pleasure spots. Soon, he felt his master's powerful arms around him.

"My pet didn't cum yet, did he?"

"No sir," Darkie panted as he looked down at himself. His own little panther cock was still rock hard. It stuck straight out in front of him, short but a little thick. His master gently caressed the barbs near his tip, making him gasp in pleasure.

"Your mistress said if you were a disappointment, you were not to be allowed to cum."

"Yes sir."

"Well, I think you've earned it for being such a good little cockslut. You like having my cock in your ass, don't you boy?"

"Yes sir," Darkie blushed hard, still loving the feel of the thick maleness buried under his tail.

"Then, cum for me boy. I want to feel you cum with my cock inside you. I want you to stroke your little prick till your body quivers with your climax. Do you understand?"

"Yes master," Darkie sighed, grateful that the fun was not over yet even though he didn't really need the release of orgasm. Tonight had already fulfilled him so much; he just wanted to keep his master's cock inside him as long as possible.

Darkie reached down and began to stroke his hard little cock. He mewed happily as he squeezed himself, teasing his own barbs and beginning to pump his shaft up and down. He knew he couldn't last very long as he was painfully aroused and his master's thick cockhead was still pressing hard against his prostate. He leaned his head to the side, submissively bearing his neck to his master.

Sinclair took the hint and bit down on the side of the panther's neck. His pet moaned, his black paw stroking his little pink cathood faster and faster now.

"That's it boy, cum for your master. I want to see that little cock spurting all over your belly."

Sinclair teased him along as he nibbled and bit on his neckfur. When he reached down and tugged gently on the panther's balls, that was too much. He held his pet's black ball sack gently but firmly in his strong paw as it drew up close to the feline's body.

Darkie yowled as he his balls rose up tightly to his body, his master's thick cock gave him a final nudge inside and sent him over the edge. Ropes of white, feline cum sprayed from his cock-tip, splattering all over his black bellyfur. As he came, his body clenched down. Behind him, his master groaned as his tight insides squeezed the thick wolfcock that was still hard and locked inside him. Darkie moaned again as it felt so much thicker when he squeezed down. He gave it another voluntary squeeze as his climax ebbed. He slowly stroked his shaft, milking out the last of his load. He looked down to see the beads of white cum standing out against the midnight-black of his fur.

"Thank you, sir," Darkie panted.

"My pleasure," the wolf cooed into his ear.

The two stayed like that a while, trying to regain their strength to move again. Sinclair then dropped his temporary pet off at the Raven again, passing his leash and full camera back over to his mistress, who smiled gratefully as she took them.

"So, what now pretty wolf? Another hunt?" She purred at him.

Sinclair yawned a little. "Nah, I'm calling it a night. Training your pet took a lot out of me, not that it wasn't very rewarding though."

She smiled as he returned to his car, licking her lips as she took in his tight rump.

"One day, I'll have that ass," she said, partly to herself.

"Yes, mistress," Darkie cooed from his place at her feet, also watching intently as the wolf walked away.

3. Trevor and Jamie

Trevor's parking brake made a scrunch as he pulled up on the lever and turned off his car. He looked out at the impressive house he'd parked in front of. The fox gave a low whistle as he took it in.

Originally, he was supposed to meet the rabbit Sinclair had set him up with at the "Dewdrop Inn", which was known locally as 'Hotel Yiff' or the 'Sleep n Fuck', but the bunny had e-mailed him last night with the news that his parents were out of town for a week so he had the house to himself.

So, here he was in one of the richest parts of town and feeling quite out of place. Luckily, darkness had already fallen so the shy fox didn't worry too much about being seen as he rung the doorbell.

"Hi," the bunny said as he opened the door.

"Um, hello," Trevor replied as he shyly waved.

The rabbit beckoned Trevor inside and chuckled as he turned around to lock the door.

Trevor looked the bunny up and down as he took off his shoes. The rabbit was quite a bit taller than he was and had an even slimmer build. His fur was mostly grey, except for the odd speck of darker fur here and there. When he turned around, Trevor saw his black t-shirt had greenish text on the front that said "How far down does the rabbit hole go?"

"Hey, that's one of my favourite movies," Trevor pointed, giggling a little.

"Yeah, but when I'm wearing it, it takes on a whole new meaning," he replied with a wink.

"Oh," Trevor blushed a bit as he realized what the bunny meant.

"So, um, what do I call you?" he asked, to break the silence.

"Oh, everyone just calls me Bunny, that's fine."

"Um okay, well I'm Trevor…"

"I know silly," Bunny said. "Your mate's told me all about you. He was right about you being a cutie."

The fox blushed a little under his fur as Bunny led the way from the foyer into the living room.

"Well, he's not really…ummm…he's never called me his mate before."

"Oh?" Bunny thought for a bit. "Well, I guess he didn't really say that, I just kinda assumed. He seems quite fond of you."

Trevor followed, not quite sure what to do yet. He timidly approached one of the overstuffed chairs and sat the bag Sinclair had packed for him next to it.

"So, I'm supposed to show you how to top, am I?" Bunny smiled at the shy fox.

Trevor blushed under his fur, "Um, yeah I guess so…"

Bunny smiled and walked over to Trevor and nuzzled his neckfur gently.

"Its really easy foxy, you just do to me all the things you like to have done to you. Subs sometimes make the best doms."

Bunny gently bumped noses with the slightly shorter fox, "Don't worry, I can teach you."

"Really? You don't mind?"

"Nah," Bunny chuckled as he rubbed the fox's crotch, "You can learn a lot from a bunny."

"Let's start by getting undressed so I can show you the pool," Bunny said with a wink.

Before coming over tonight, Bunny had told Trevor on the phone that his parent's house had a heated outdoor swimming pool that he loved to skinny dip in whenever they weren't around. Trevor was a little nervous about the thought of swimming in the nude in an outdoor pool, but he wanted to be a little adventurous so he'd agreed to come over and try it out.

Bunny had walked up close to him and was pawing at his crotch a little more now. Trevor giggled and turned a little, letting Bunny open the lacings in the front of his pants. The fox slipped his shirt off and tossed it on the floor next to the chair.

"Ooh, nice chest foxy."

"Thanks," Trevor shyly accepted the compliment. "You're really cute," he added.

The rabbit looked up with a grin as he opened Trevor's pants. He began to tug gently, coaxing them down. The fox obligingly straightened his back and slipped them down, eventually sliding them all the way off to join his shirt on the floor. He smirked as he saw Bunny looking at his thick sheath.

"Nothing underneath, very nice foxy," he licked his lips as he thought about what lay hidden in the fox's downy white sheath.

Bunny sat up for a moment and stripped his shirt off, also tossing it carelessly on the living room rug.

"Ooh," Trevor gasped as he saw the rabbit's trim form. He was even slimmer than Trevor himself, his muscles were held close to his frame which gave him a sleek but strong look. The fox also noticed the pants Bunny was wearing. He leaned forward and gently stroked the lapine's leg. "Neat," he said as he gently petted the soft, black velvet.

"Thanks, I call them my "fuck me" pants," Bunny grinned as he pushed them off. They hit the ground with a near-silent swoosh as they slid down his slender feminine thighs.

The fox grinned at that comment as he quickly pulled off his socks and stood back up. Now that the two were completely naked, Bunny gestured to the large glass doors leading to the patio and pool area.

"Shall we," he asked with a smile and Trevor let him lead the way outside. He licked his lips as he followed, watching the rabbit's small, round bottom moving under his white tail puff. He found himself starting to think like a top for the first time that evening and realized maybe it wouldn't be as hard as he thought to get in the mood to give rather than receive.

Bunny wasted no time in diving into the pool. Trevor looked around a little nervously as he approached the water. It was already dark outside, but the pool had lights on under the water so he could see Bunny clearly. The pool area was fenced in so he wasn't worried about anyone seeing from the road or sneaking up behind the house, but the fourth side of the pool was bordered by Bunny's neighbour's house.

"Don't worry," the rabbit said as he surfaced and saw where the fox was looking, "There aren't any windows on that side of their house. No one will see us."

Trevor wasn't used to the luxury of a heated swimming pool so he stepped in slowly, starting with one toe. He gasped in surprised as he realized how warm the water actually was. It felt almost like warm bathwater and he quickly immersed himself fully.

Trevor leaned back against one side of the pool and sighed happily. He let his legs go limp and slowly move back and forth under the warm water.

"Wow, you were right. This is really nice," he said with a smile.

Trevor watched as Bunny swam back and forth in front of him. The fox enjoyed watching the rabbit's wet slender body as he slid through the water. He licked his lips as he closely watched Bunny's long, slim cock and low-hanging balls as he came to a stop just in front of him.

"I see you're enjoying this," the rabbit said with a smile, eyeing something below the water line.

Trevor looked down and sure enough, his foxhood was extended from his sheath and fully hard. He murred happily and moved gently back and forth, allowing his firm erection to sweep through the warm water. He'd taken baths that had resulted in an erection before of course, but the feeling of being in enough warm water to float and let his cock drift in the warm in front of him felt amazing and very different from being naked in a bath or shower. This was his first time skinny dipping as he'd never gone to any of the camps where "interesting" things happened when he was a kid. He was enjoying exploring the new feelings when Bunny floated up to him and pressed his naked body against him.

The fox moaned as he felt the rabbit's long, hard cock sliding up and down against his own erection. Although he couldn't really see it in the water, he could feel he was leaking precum already and was really surprised that being naked in this warm pool, even with a very hot companion, had gotten him so aroused so quickly. Trevor held Bunny a little closer and slowly stroked his back and eventually reached down to cup the smooth curve of his butt. Bunny's furry body quivered with the touch as his own paws explored the sexy fox's body. Trevor moaned and leaked more slick precum as the lapine's paw reached between his legs and gave his dangling balls a gentle squeeze.

The two rubbed their slick, furry bodies against each other for several minutes, quickly becoming more and more aroused. Bunny winked, took a deep breath and slipped under the water. The feeling was so sudden and indescribably pleasurable as Bunny's muzzle slipped around Trevor's fully erect cock that the fox gasped out loud.

"Ohhhh," he moaned long as the rabbit began to suck him off under the water. He could only whimper and gently play with the rabbit's ears as the short, white muzzle bobbed up and down his thick length.

The fox's lower half floated weightlessly in the soothing water as the bunny's long tongue lapped up and down his thick fox-cock. He let himself drift on the sensations until he began to feel the pressure building at the base of his cock and he knew he would not be able to hold back much longer. With a great deal of reluctance, Trevor slowly pulled the rabbit off his cock.

"You've got to stop now," he panted, "If you keep going I'm going to cum and I…really want to mount you."

Trevor found himself surprised to be saying that, but he really meant it. He was definitely enjoying having another fur being his submissive for a change and he could fully appreciate how much pleasure his partner got out of dominating him.

"Really?" Bunny asked as he reached down and gripped the rock hard foxhood under the water.

Trevor moaned as the rabbit massaged his thick length.

"Ooh, now this is a nice surprise," Bunny said as he gently slid his fingers up and down Trevor's cock.

Trevor blushed, "What's so surprising about it?"

Bunny gave him a sly grin before replying, "Well, I ordered a toy once that was modeled after a fox and it was really tiny. I ended up trading it with a friend for a much larger one."

"Oh…"

"Yeah, I thought foxes were tiny, but you're definitely enough to fill me up," Bunny murred happily as he gave Trevor a slightly firmer squeeze and then turned around.

Trevor took a sharp intake of breath as Bunny pressed his tail up against his rock hard cock. His foxhood slid up and down along the rabbit's slick fur and his thick tip pressed into the smooth furless spot under his fluffy, white tail. Trevor gripped the rabbit about the waist and turned them both around so he was holding Bunny against the edge of the pool. The rabbit braced himself against the wall as Trevor pushed against him, grinding their bodies together. Trevor's precum was slick enough even in the water to help his cocktip press into the ring of the bunny's tight tail.

Trevor ground his cock up and down along the underside of Bunny's tail for several minutes while reaching around and stroking the rabbit's long, hard cock before Bunny hauled himself out of the pool and insisted they go inside and do it right now.

The fox's cock throbbed with need as he watched the nude rabbit hop out of the pool and skip through the warm, night air. All he could focus on was the white fluffy tail and the way that gorgeous rump moved under it as the rabbit walked. Trevor got out of the pool and followed Bunny inside.

The pair stood in the living room and caressed the slick, wet fur of each other's bodies. Both whimpered and moaned with need as cocks were stroked, balls were fondled and butts were gently squeezed. Both were raging hard by the time the rabbit leaned back, baring his throat for his new master. The fox's predatory side took over and he leaned in to gently nip at his prey's neck. The rabbit's whole body shivered with lust as he gave himself over to the fox.

Trevor released his prey's neck and the bunny gently panted as they nuzzled each other's tender neckfur. The fox remembered what Bunny had said earlier about doing to him what he liked to have done to him. Standing there soaking wet, naked and vulnerable, Trevor knew just what to do.

He held the rabbit by one paw as he sat down on the chair he'd put his bag next to earlier. As he pulled the bunny along, the rabbit quickly got the idea and laid himself down over Trevor's knee. They were both far too turned on not to fool around now. They both knew it so Bunny was ready for it and wanting it badly when Trevor's paw began to spank his wet, exposed bottom hard and fast. The rabbit gasped and moaned as the fox spanked him. Usually when playing like this he had a slow warmup, but not tonight. Tonight the smacks on his bare bottom stung hard and came quickly and he loved it. His slick body writhed against Trevor's as the fox's paw swatted each cheek one after the other. He moaned with lust and pushed his rump up into Trevor's paw, wanting to feel it even more. As he pushed his bottom up, his furry cheeks spread apart slightly, giving the fox a clear view of the treasure that lay in wait for him.

Bunny moaned as the fox growled slightly. He whimpered as the spanking stopped for a moment and he realized he could hear Trevor rustling in his bag on the floor for something. He didn't know what the fox was doing, but the anticipation made his cock throb with need and he could feel it bump against the fox's erection under him. He spread his legs slightly, exposing his tailhole more for the fox as he thought about having that thick, vulpine member splitting him open.

Soon, the hard smacks on his exposed bottom started again, only much harder than before. He yelped as the hairbrush smacked hard against his wet furry rump. He knew he would be getting nice and red under his light grey and white fur back there. His balls bounced up and down enticingly as he squirmed on the fox's lap.

"Ahhh Trevor, mount me," he begged, his voice almost choked with lust.

Trevor paddled the rabbit's needy bottom for another few minutes before standing up slowly and tossing the brush aside. The bunny quickly got on the floor on all fours. He parted his legs just right to show off his low-hanging balls. The reddened cheeks of his small, round bottom were parted just enough for Trevor to see the tight pink hole under the rabbit's fluffy tail.

Bunny looked back at him with need in his eyes, his small muzzle was open slightly and he panted gently. The sight was such that even a submissive, effeminate fox like Trevor was filled with predatory lust and the desire to mount quickly and claim the prey for his own.

In a flash, Trevor was on Bunny's back, teasing him by gently dry-humping against his tailhole. The rabbit moaned as he felt the fox's thick cocktip, slick with precum, sliding back and forth against his hole.

"Oh, sir. Don't tease me, mount me...please," the rabbit begged.

Trevor exhaled as he pressed his foxhood against Bunny's opening. He was surprised by how warm it felt and how hard his cock was at the thought of mounting Bunny. He held himself there a moment, just gently pressing his tip against the willing submissive. Bunny helped him out by pushing back against the prodding foxcock. Trevor moaned as he felt the tight tailhole opening up and swallowing his cock. He looked down to see his tip disappearing under the rabbit's small fluffy tail. Bunny moaned as the fox's thick tip began to spread him open. Trevor found it incredibly hot to see his thick foxhood slowly sliding into Bunny's small, round rear. The rabbit seemed too small and thin to be able to take him easily, but Bunny's moans and the way he was whimpering told him otherwise.

"Ohh, mount me foxy," he begged again as Trevor gently teased him.

Trevor's long buried instincts as a predator species came over him at the sight of his own cock slowly opening up the willing prey's tight rear for him. The fox gave a little growl, not quite as impressive as Sinclair's but to the bunny under him it was all he needed to hear to make him quiver with submissive joy under a dominant predator. Trevor thrust forward hard and hilted every inch of his thick foxhood under the rabbit's small tail.

"Ohhh, yeah," Bunny groaned to himself as Trevor pushed his shoulders down and plunged into him even deeper.

The little fox held onto Bunny and began to hump him hard and fast as his instincts took over. He growled and held his prey tightly as he mounted him as hard as he could. Trevor had no idea it could feel this good to be on top and the rabbit was so tight it made his eyes water. He bit down on the bunny's shoulder and held on as his hips thrust out of control.

Trevor was going on instinct alone, but Bunny was more used to this. He pushed back into the fox's wild thrusts so he could feel the thick foxcock as deeply as possible. His own long slender member dripped precum onto the floor as Trevor pounded his prostate again and again. Bunny gripped the carpet and pushed back to keep Trevor's cock as deep as possible.

For a first timer, the fox was doing a good job hitting all the right spots under Bunny's tail. Although, as hung as the fox was it wasn't hard to miss. The initial pain of being entered had quickly faded and now, the slender young rabbit only felt the pleasure of being taken hard and fast. Luckily, he was experienced and could hold off his own pleasure so the night didn't end too quickly. He could tell that the fox wasn't going to last long, but he hoped he could tease another climax out of Trevor later on.

Trevor cried out and gripped his prey tightly as he came inside the tight tailhole he'd been brutally riding. He filled the rabbit up with several long spurts of fox cum before collapsing on Bunny's back and panting into his neckfur. Under him, Bunny was grinning mischievously as he squeezed down his passage on the fox's sensitive member. Trevor whimpered as the tailhole tightened down on him. Being over stimulated, it felt good and bad at the same time. He gave Bunny some of his own medicine and pushed forward again as deep as he could. His cock was still nice and hard and the rabbit moaned loudly as it pressed him deep inside.

"Oh...wow," Trevor panted after a few minutes.

"Did the foxy have fun?" Bunny asked as he wiggled his rear against Trevor's groin.

Trevor responded by grinding his crotch against Bunny's rear. The submissive rabbit moaned as the thick foxcock pushed deep inside him again. With this encouragement, the fox continued to tease his new friend. His paws roamed around and caressed Bunny's chestfur as he gently humped into him. Bunny squealed a little as Trevor found and squeezed his nipples.

Soon, the fox's paws had wandered farther down over his partner's slim stomach and between his legs. Bunny moaned again as Trevor began to slowly caress the rabbit's long, hard cock. He slowly traced every inch of the rabbit's member with his soft paw. The slow teasing was maddening, but Bunny didn't say a word. He let Trevor do what he wanted to him even though his balls were aching for release after the spanking, rough mounting and soft caressing on his cock.

Trevor was getting bolder again. He was gently stroking up and down Bunny's whole length while his other paw had snuck farther back between the rabbit's shapely thighs to gently tug on the Bunny's low-hanging balls. He continued to push his foxhood in and out of the squirming rabbit's tailhole and occasionally pushed all the way in as he was enjoying hearing Bunny moan whenever he did that.

Bunny had thought he could hold off his own climax, but he wasn't able to resist the gentle caressing of the fox's soft paws on his cock. His body shivered and his back arched as Trevor slowly stroked him from base to tip while gently tugging on his full balls. He started to pant, his eyes watering as the pleasure started to overwhelm him.

"Tug them a little harder..I'm...so...close," the rabbit gasped.

Trevor realized the rabbit liked things a little rough like he did so he began to pull and squeeze the dangling balls in his paw while his other paw slid quickly up and down the bunny's long shaft. While pawing his prey off, Trevor continued to gently hump against the rabbit's abused bottom. When he shoved his thick foxhood all the way in while tugging down on Bunny's balls, the rabbit groaned deeply and came hard. His body shivered with the stimulation as Trevor milked him dry.

The fox smiled with satisfaction as watched Bunny's cock spurting all over the living room carpet. He wondered if he should've caught the rabbit's load before it got everywhere, but he doubted Bunny cared much about cleaning up his parent's house at the moment.

Trevor gave his new friend's cock a long, firm squeeze along the whole length to milk out the last of his cum. When he was sure the bunny was done, he sat back and leaned against the chair. Bunny was pulled with him and ended up sitting on Trevor's lap with the fox's cock balls-deep under his tail. Bunny's cock sprung up again from the new pressure he felt deep inside.

Trevor's ears lowered as he peaked around to see Bunny's face, "So how'd I do?" he shyly asked.

Bunny grinned and squeezed down on the foxcock deep under his tail, "I don't think I really have to teach you anything foxy. So, how'd you like topping?"

Trevor giggled a little, "I never thought I'd like it so much. It was fun to be in charge for a while, but I mostly liked it when you moaned a lot."

As Trevor's cock shrunk back down into his sheath, Bunny got up and sat next to him. The two nuzzled for a little before Trevor asked a question.

"Um, so what is your name?"

Bunny grinned and licked his nose, "Why so curious foxy?"

Trevor laughed a little and confessed he'd told Sinclair he would find out.

"Jamie", the rabbit replied with a giggle as he stood up.

"Cool," the fox beamed from his place on the floor as he watched Jamie pick up some clothes from his couch.

Trevor gasped in appreciation as the bunny slipped on a pair of slightly transparent black panties. Jamie walked over to the stairs and looked back at Trevor, "You want to come up to my room now?"

The question was posed almost innocently, except for the sly wiggle of the rabbit's tail above his panty-covered rump.

The fox wondered how much the bunny's tail could take, but he figured he'd probably find out as he picked up the bag of toys Sinclair had packed for him and followed Jamie upstairs. This was going to be a fun night.

4. Sinclair and Trevor

Sinclair sighed as he sat down. He twitched his ears to get the water out as he tied his robe closed. After bringing Darkie back to the Raven and to his Mistress, he'd come home and taken a shower. Now, it was time to relax a bit. He smiled as he took a swig of water and wondered how Trevor's night had gone with Bunny. He expected he'd get an e-mail from the fox in the morning about it. Poor Trevor would probably be so exhausted; he'd just go home to bed.

The wolf looked up as he heard a knock at the door. He grunted as he heaved himself out of his comfortable chair. Sinclair glanced at the clock as he unlocked the door. He wondered who the hell was coming by this late.

"Hi wolfie," Trevor beamed as the door opened.

"Hey, I'm surprised to see you," Sinclair replied as he stepped aside to let the fox in. "I would have thought you'd go home and collapse."

"Nah," Trevor shrugged off his jacket, "I wanted to see ya. In fact, I was hoping I could spend the night." He turned to look at Sinclair as the wolf was closing the door. "If you don't mind, wolfie."

Sinclair smiled, feeling a stirring in his sheath for a moment.

"I was thinking of going to bed, but I'm not that tired," he replied with a grin.

"Heh, evil wolf," Trevor smiled as he kicked off his shoes.

By now, Sinclair had crossed the gap between them and was gently caressing Trevor's shoulders. He closed his eyes for a moment and breathed in his scent. Trevor sighed and leaned back against him.

"You know, people think we're mates," he said thoughtfully, almost to himself.

"Really?" Sinclair paused for a moment, "That's funny, eh?"

Trevor was silent for a moment, just thinking and enjoying the warmth of his frequent bed-mate against him.

"Yeah, I guess it is," he smiled and made his way into the living room, slowly unbuckling his belt as he walked.

Sinclair walked past him and sat down on the couch. The fox turned and looked at him curiously.

"I want a good seat for the show, foxy."

Trevor smiled, "Oh, you want a show hmm?"

The wolf licked his lips, grinning as wolfishly as possible. "You know it foxy."

"Say the magic words then," Trevor leaned forward, his paws on his knees. He grinned and swayed his hips slightly.

Sinclair's expression hardened, "Strip now, fox." He ordered with a steely tone.

"Oooh, yes sir," Trevor moaned, his foxcock throbbed with lust as he felt the wonderful submissive feelings wash over him.

The slim fox began by running his paws slowly up his leather-clad thighs and over the growing bulge at his groin; he whined softly and squeezed himself through his pants. He grinned, knowing what this was doing to the watching wolf. He ran his paws up over his chest and stretched his arms out, posing a little. Trevor started with his shirt. He gripped the bottom of it and slowly pulled it up, peeling the tight shirt off like a second skin. He saw Sinclair exhale suddenly as he revealed the fluffy white fur of his trim belly. He removed the rest of his shirt slowly, making sure to give his nipples a little tweak as he raised it over his chest. Next he pulled it over his head, shaking his head so his headfur got ruffled around as the shirt slipped down one arm. Trevor dangled it from his fingertips for a moment before it dropped silently to the floor.

Next, the sultry vulpine ran his paws over his bare chest and belly, again moving down to caress the outline of his sheath when he reached his pants. He turned around and bent over, running his paws up the backs of his thighs and over his perfectly round rump. He looked behind him while raising his tail.

"Like what you see, sir?"

Sinclair growled from the couch. "You naughty little foxslut, just wait till you get over here."

Trevor smiled wickedly and ran his fingertips over his crack, clearly outlined through the tight leather pants. Next, he began to work at the lacings on the front of his pants. His nervous fingers opened them up quickly and he felt the leather loosen around his waist. Trevor closed his eyes and slowly lowered his pants. He gasped a little as his tail slipped free and he felt the cool air on his bare rear. He let the pants down just enough to reveal his red-furred rump. He bent over and spread his legs, knowing that dominant males found the little bit of white fur that ran up between his cheeks and under his tail to be very alluring. He smiled as he imagined Sinclair's cock, aching and hard inside that loose robe.

He turned slowly, standing up straight again. He still held his pants up with one paw so they covered his groin. He leaned back a little, making his crotch jut out towards his audience. With a sly vulpine grin, Trevor slowly moved his paw aside, holding his pants at their sides. The thick tip of his hard foxcock was now visible. He slipped his pants down the rest of the way. They made a soft thump as they hit the floor and pooled around his ankles. He stood there a moment, fully revealed. He leaned his shoulders back a little and cupped his white-furred balls in one paw. Trevor moaned a little as he rolled them around and squeezed his long, thick shaft with his other paw. He was surprised at how aroused he was so soon after an intense mating. His foxcock was already leaking precum. He stepped out of his pants, being sure to turn his legs so they fully revealed the insides of his slender thighs.

"Good boy," Sinclair said softly, "Now come here, little fox."

Trevor put his head down, looking up at his master with his bright green eyes, and walked slowly towards the wolf on the couch.

Sinclair took Trevor's paw gently in his and leaned up as he gently pulled the fox close to him. He whispered softly in the fox's ear.

"Get over my knee foxy."

Trevor moaned, the very sound of the wolf's voice made his body quiver with pleasure. "Yes, sir," he barely whispered as he lay down over the wolf's strong lap. He sighed with complete contentment once he felt the familiar feel of Sinclair's strong thighs under his naked body. He felt incredibly vulnerable lying bare to his fur over the lap of a powerful predator who could do anything he wanted to him, and he loved it. Strangely, he always felt safe like this. The wolf's scent was all around him, it was a thick, masculine smell that drove him wild with desire and calmed his wildness at the same time. He knew this wolf would never hurt him. He knew Sinclair would spank his bottom till it glowed as red as his fur, he would mount him hard, fast and deep with his perfect lupine cock and tie him with his thick knot, but he would never do anything he didn't want to happen. In some subconscious way, Trevor realized he could spend forever lying over this wolf's knee and be perfectly happy and safe.

Sinclair looked down at the wonder of vulpine beauty lying over him. He saw Trevor differently in the dim half-light of his apartment. He began to gently caress Trevor's back, softly scritching with his claws. He smiled as the little fox moaned softly. He realized he had been gently caressing Trevor's fur for a long time now. Normally, in this position, he'd have had the urge to give that gorgeous rump a few good slaps to warm it up by now. He felt differently tonight though and he couldn't place why. He opened his muzzle, about to speak, but not sure what to say.

"Trevor—"

"Mmm, this feels good wolfie," Trevor mumbled sleepily as he nuzzled at Sinclair's leg.

Sinclair smiled down at Trevor again, moving down a little farther and beginning to gently caress his rump. Trevor sighed happily and raised his tail a little. Sinclair wondered if he meant to do that or if it was instinctual as he continued to rub and scritch the little fox's rear. He ran one finger slowly along the white fur that ran between Trevor's cheeks. Trevor moaned again, his body shivering. The big wolf sighed as he felt the fox's rock hard erection rubbing against his thigh.

"Trevor…I," he started to say when the fox turned and looked up at him with a dreamy expression.

"What is it wolfie?"

That was when Sinclair did something the fox wasn't expecting. He picked the smaller canid up and kissed him full on the muzzle. Trevor was surprised for a moment, but soon moaned and parted his lips, opening himself up for the wolf's deep kiss. He felt his lupine lover moving him. Soon, he was crouching over Sinclair's legs. He reached inside the wolf's robe as they kissed. Trevor's soft paws scritched and caressed the wolf's broad chest, instinctively moving down to part the loose robe.

Both furs moaned and growled gently as Sinclair's robe opened and they felt their bodies against each other suddenly. Sinclair ran his paws up and down Trevor's back as the fox rubbed down his belly. The kiss suddenly intensified even more when Trevor leaned forward slightly and the two male members pressed together, the tender flesh of each rubbing against each other. The long deep kiss went on as both furs writhed against each other, their hot bodies rubbing together. To each it felt as if they were truly exploring the other's body for the first time even though they had mated often.

"Oh gods, mate with me please. I want you in me," Trevor gasped in his partner's ear.

Sinclair didn't speak. He looked long into the fox's eyes and saw the need and the want there. There was so much in those deep eyes, he realized as he slowly lifted the fox's body up. Trevor groaned wantonly as his foxhood rubbed through the wolf's muscled stomach. He whimpered as Sinclair's soft fur teased his erect maleness. He bit his lower lip as he felt the wolf's cockhead slipping under his hanging balls and nestling comfortably between his cheeks. Soon, it was nuzzling insistently at his tight entrance. Trevor thought for a moment that he wasn't lubed up, but he didn't care. The little fox bit his lip and leaned forward, sniffing deeply. The wolf's lust-filled smell made him moan wantonly, feeding the fire of his need to be taken by this strong predator. He realized the wolf wasn't moving, he was just holding him gently. Trevor licked his cheek tenderly and slowly lowered himself, squeezing his eyes shut as Sinclair's thick, unlubed cockhead pushed roughly into his tight foxhole. He moaned as the wolf's cockhead popped in him fully. He slowly sat down on his partner's lap, feeling the long, hard shaft sliding deep inside.

Sinclair held the little fox tightly in his arms, hugging him to his chest and nuzzling his neck.

"Trevor, you're amazing," he gasped as he nuzzled the little fox's cheek.

Under his fur, Trevor blushed happily as he nuzzled back,

shivering a little as Sinclair began to nibble gently at his neck. Soon, the wolf was kissing him again. Trevor moaned as he felt his lover's paw tightly gripping his erection as they kissed. The fox began to move slowly up and down on Sinclair's lap. As his tailhole adjusted to the wolf's cock in him, he humped his own thick shaft into Sinclair's soft-furred paw.

Sinclair broke the kiss and sat back to watch the fox on his lap. He smiled as he took in the sight of the young, slim fox riding his wolfhood. He alternated between squeezing and gently teasing the foxcock in his paw while his other paw reached behind Trevor to grip the base of his tail. He leaned forward and nuzzled Trevor's chest and took one of the fox's nipples into his muzzle and bit gently. Trevor's body shivered, but Sinclair wasn't sure if it was the little love bite on his nipple or because he was now pushing his wolfhood into the fox teasingly slow.

"Cum for me, pretty fox," Sinclair growled to his vulpine lover as he licked and nuzzled at Trevor's chest.

"I'm...so...close," Trevor whimpered.

Sinclair groaned as the fox's tailhole squeezed his cock like a vise. He leaned down and took the tip of Trevor's foxhood into his muzzle. His long, slick tongue wrapped around the cocktip and squeezed. The fox squirmed in his lap and began to thrust more insistently into his muzzle which also made Trevor drive himself down onto the wolf's cock even harder.

Sinclair moaned and sucked the fox's thick cock hard. The stimulation of the thick wolf cock pumping in his tight rear and the teasing and sucking on his rock hard cock was too much for the fox to take. He held on as long as he could, hoping to feel the wolf cum inside him, but he couldn't last as Sinclair was holding back on purpose.

Trevor's slim thighs tightened around Sinclair's lap and he came hard, suddenly filling his partner's muzzle with his vulpine cum. Trevor sat down hard on Sinclair's cock as he rode out his powerful climax. He took the wolfcock as deep as he could before Sinclair shoved it just a little deeper to completely milk his body dry. Trevor collapsed against the strong wolf as he panted. The fox soon realized that the wolf was still rock hard and hadn't cum yet.

"Why didn't you...y'know?" Trevor asked softly.

The wolf caressed his fox's muzzle softly, which caused Trevor to smile and give his paw a little lick. Sinclair smiled as he replied, "I was having too much fun watching you, fox."

"Silly wolf," Trevor said as he grinned. "Do you want me to help you with this?" He asked as he playfully squeezed his rump down on the wolf's erection.

"Let's try something different," Sinclair responded as he gently lifted the smaller mammal off his lap.

Trevor squirmed as the thick cock suddenly slid out of him. Sinclair picked him up and gently laid him down on the soft, furry rug he had in front of his couch. The wolf crouched over Trevor's body with his thighs around the fox's chest. He slowly leaned forward and let his thick wolfcock slowly press against Trevor's chest.

"Mmm, your fur is so soft, fox."

Sinclair moved his cock back and forth slowly, allowing the soft red fur to tease his tender cocktip. His precum left a small sticky spot on Trevor's chest. He leaned down and held the fox's paws above his head as they kissed. The pair looked into each other's eyes.

"Do you want to cum on me, sir?"

Sinclair just growled a little and nibbled the edge of Trevor's left ear. This made the fox moan and squirm a little. He pushed his chest up a bit, enveloping the wolf's hard, red cock in his soft fur.

"Do it," he gasped as the thought of the wolf cumming on him made him hard again, "Mark me with your seed, wolfie."

Sinclair held his lover down and began to slowly hump his wolfhood along Trevor's chest. The teasing softness of the fox's fur was almost too much to take. The sensation felt incredible, almost as good as taking Trevor's tight bottom. His eyes watered as the gentle teasing along his entire length overwhelmed him.

"Uh, I'm going to cum all over you, sexy fox." He choked as he his cock swelled. He felt close to bursting any second. His balls bounced back and forth as he humped himself faster along the fox's incredible furry body.

"Yes, that's it wolf. Cover me in your cum, please!" Trevor begged.

Sinclair made a groan like Trevor had never heard before and suddenly, he felt wetness on his cheek from the first spurt of the wolf's climax. His attention was focused on the tip of the wolf's cock as it pushed its way through his fur. The tip was so close to his face as the thick cock swelled and unleashed the rest of its load onto him. Trevor smiled in ecstasy as he felt the hot, heavy ropes of cum hitting his fur. The wolf cum dripped off his cheek and coated his neck. As Sinclair humped the last few spurts out, the fox's upper chest became sticky and wet too. Trevor's body quivered with a kind of submissive mental orgasm as he felt his face and neck being coated by his lover's seed.

Sinclair panted for a few minutes as Trevor looked up at him. Eventually, the wolf released his paws and Trevor sat up a little. The two kissed deeply once more.

"That was..."

"Wonderful."

They kissed and nuzzled for several minutes. Sinclair caressed Trevor's cheek again, which the fox clearly loved.

"Trevor..."

"Yes?" the young fox asked eagerly.

The wolf continued to caress Trevor's cheek with one paw while holding one of the fox's paws with the other.

"Trevor, I"

"Yes, wolf."

The fox leaned forward a bit as the two locked eyes for a long moment.

The wolf's lips began to part as he looked at the fox. He opened his mouth to speak. Trevor was on pins and needles waiting to hear the wolf say it...

Sinclair's eyes darted over to his coffee table as a shrill beeping filled the room.

"Dammit," he growled as he snatched his cell phone off the table. His expression turned grave as he saw the number that was calling him.

"Sinclair here."

Trevor's ears drooped a little as he watched his wolf lover's expression change for the worse.

"I'll be right there," Sinclair grunted.

"You have to go," Trevor stated as the wolf looked at him.

"I'm sorry to run off like this."

Trevor smiled and put on his best face to hide how he felt. He didn't want to force this moment now, it had to happen naturally. Maybe when Sinclair came home, they'd have time again.

"It's okay wolfie, I know you're needed. Go be a hero," he said as he smiled and hugged his lover. "I'll be here when you get back," he whispered.

Sinclair smiled and found that comforting. "I don't know when I'll be home," he said as he stood. "You're welcome to stay though," he continued as he rummaged around for his clothes.

He pulled on the same clothes he'd worn during the day. Trevor shifted a little nervously as he watched the wolf check his gun before holstering it. He started for the door when Trevor suddenly called him back.

Sinclair turned to see the fox was holding his wallet. Trevor tossed it to him. It spun in the air and Sinclair's badge caught the light for a moment before the wolf deftly caught it.

"Thanks fox," he smiled.

After the wolf had left, Trevor idly picked at the drying cum on his chestfur as he walked back to the couch. He pulled Sinclair's robe around him and curled up on the couch. He felt safe again, surrounded by the scent of his wolf as he fell asleep.

A Trick of the Light

The lights pulsed rhythmically. Bodies moved in time with the music. The room was dark, hot and full of furry bodies moving together.

A good-sized gray wolf stood off to the side, just watching the room for a while.

He was at one of the largest costume parties in town. In fact, furs from all over the country came to this one, and it was infamous. He had only heard about it at the last minute though. He'd gotten the basics from a friend who knew somebody who hung out with someone else that had gone to the party once years ago. The wolf's friend had been rather vague in his description of the events, possibly because they were both a bit out of it when the discussion came up.

Suffice it to say, the wolf had spent his fair share of time just watching to see how things were done here. Supposedly you could find whatever you were looking for for a good time at this particular gathering. This was known as a party for playful furs and was held annually. But it was only a good time if you knew how to play it right. Or so he'd heard. He'd wall-flowered all night so far, but he hoped to get lucky tonight. He scanned the crowd in hopes of seeing someone that interested him. He hated having to rely on his vision alone, but with the amount of smoke in the air, not to mention the abundance of strong perfumes and colognes, he couldn't pick much up by smell tonight. He shrugged and squinted slightly into the darkness, hoping that his lupine night vision would be enough to find what he was looking for.

He stretched a bit, rubbed an itchy spot on his back against the wall and continued to watch the crowd. He was a fur with quite a large frame, muscular and tall. He was quite imposing looking, even if a little shy sometimes. He had taken advantage of his natural attributes and chosen an appropriate costume. He was dressed as a high school jock, complete with a tight pair of jeans that emphasized his lower physique and a red and white letter jacket. The jacket showed its age a little since it was once his dad's, but seemed to fit okay. He looked a far cry from his usual self. He was a typically shy, mid-twenties call-center tech, and much more used to khakis and polo shirts than his current outfit.

A particularly hard-thumping song had started up and the whole crowd moved wildly. Slowly, however, the center of the group parted as if by magic. The wolf leaned forward to see that the crowd had parted to show off a fur dancing up a sensual storm. The fur, a beautiful red vixen, was dressed as a Catholic schoolgirl. How perfect is that, the wolf asked himself. The wolf's eyes started at the floor, on the small black shoes that moved gracefully across the dance floor and followed the supple curves of her lower legs, covered with long, white socks. He blinked and nearly missed a flash of red-furred vulpine thigh as the fox's pleated skirt swished around in a twirl.

The wolf felt an uncomfortable thickening in his sheath as he continued to mentally undress the dancing fox. Above her swishing skirt and wonderfully curved legs, she wore a white shirt, covered by a sweater that matched the colours of her skirt. He noticed she was rather small chested, but that didn't matter. He was more of an ass-man anyway, and from what he could see, this fox had a positively delicious rear under that bushy, red tail. And those eyes were really captivating, full of sultry wanting. They flashed a sparkling blue from across the room, and connected with his for a moment.

That was when the now very aroused wolf decided to make his move. He worked his way around the dance floor, close to the wall on the side where the fox danced. As the song finished and she left the dance floor amidst some applause, he was right there to offer her a drink.

At the bar, the young fox gratefully took a tall glass of water.

"Thank you, dancing like that really gets me quite hot."

The wolf's sheath throbbed within his jeans as she spoke. He began to try and stutter out his name, too horny or too nervous to think straight.

The fox gently put a soft black-furred fingertip to his muzzle.

"Sssh, no names," the vixen whispered with a lusty tone.

As she leaned in close; he could smell her sweet perfume. "Just take me somewhere private."

He nearly came on himself as her soft cheekfur tickled his sensitive lupine ear. She took his paw in hers and led him away. He didn't stop to think until they got to the door of the men's room and the fox led him inside.

"Are you sure about this?"

"Look at the door love, it has a lock."

With a sly grin, the eager fox pulled him inside by the paw and quickly bolted the door.

"Just relax, and let me show you a good time," the vixen commanded.

Within seconds, the pair was kissing passionately. The jock wolf could feel his companion's paws pulling open his pants. Once he had stepped out of his jeans, he began to slip his jacket off, but the schoolgirl placed a paw on his shoulder and whispered,

"Leave it on, it's sexy."

He could only stand and throb as the talented vixen worked him over, teasing his maleness through his straining boxers and squeezing his tightly muscled rump.

"Oh gods," he whimpered as she gave him a little squeeze and began to slide down his boxers.

"Oooh, you're a big boy," the fox squealed with delight once the wolf's thick shaft was fully exposed in front of her muzzle. She buried her small black nose in the fur of his crotch, deeply breathing in his scent while nuzzling at the side of his shaft.

The wolf gasped and moaned, letting the beautiful fox back him up against a tiled wall. She began to nurse his cock now, flicking her tongue against his dripping tip before sucking his hard shaft into her muzzle. The wolf was overcome, he'd never heard of a girl doing something like this before. Surely, this was something that only happened in stroke mags.

Suddenly, the sensation ceased. He opened his eyes to look down at his new friend for the night.

"Am I doing good Mr. Wolf?" She asked with an impish grin, eyes glowing.

He couldn't hold himself back anymore; he had to have her now. The counter was at just the right height so he lifted her up and sat her down on it. The wolf took the fox in a deep, passionate kiss. As he kissed her, making her whimper with desire, one of his paws slipped slowly, teasingly, up her red-furred thighs and between her legs. He ran a paw lightly over her wettening panties, before slowly slipping inside to feel her…

…thick male shaft!

With a yelp, the wolf backed away quickly, leaving his very clearly male companion's huge erection peeking out under his skirt.

"What's wrong lover?" the fox asked, genuinely confused.

"Y-you're a— a male!"

The fox giggled and reached down to stroke the thick shaft that was still sticking up out of his white panties.

"Yep, it certainly feels that way. What else would I be?"

The wolf was really dumbfounded now, and waved his paws back and forth.

"I dunno, maybe a girl!" He nearly screamed.

The fox chuckled to himself. "I would have thought you knew, there aren't any girls here."

"Wh-what?"

"This is an all-male party. Didn't you know that?"

The wolf blinked repeatedly, then began to understand. The fox had started to laugh now, and the wolf felt his face grow red under his fur. His tail slowly curled around one leg, beginning to work its way up between his legs. He started to back away, not quite sure what to do. How could he have gotten so turned on by another male? He couldn't be gay, could he? He had just about reached the door and was stretching his paw out for the handle.

"Hey, what're you—" The fox cocked his head curiously. "You're not going, are you?" He asked, a measure of disappointment in his voice.

"Y-you tricked me fox."

"But, I didn't. It's not my fault! How come you came to an all gay party anyway?"

"But—" the wolf covered his muzzle and whimpered. "I'm not

gay."

The poor wolf looked a bit scared now, and the fox felt sorry for him in a way.

"Aww, it's okay sweetie. Of course you're not." The little fox had scooted off the counter now and made his way over to the wolf. "You just got a little confused is all."

"Um…yeah, that's right," the big wolf stammered as the fox took him by the paw and led him back towards the counter. "My friend told me to come here…"

The wolf allowed himself to be led by the paw. He'd thought his friend had just been drunk when he'd told the wolf about this party because he hadn't stopped giggling while giving the wolf directions. Now, he knew the real reason why.

The fox looked back over his shoulder and tried to suppress the urge to lick his lips at the sight of wolf's throbbing erection, which hadn't gotten any less rampant.

"Your costume is very…ah, convincing."

"Why, thank you wolfie," the fox said flirtatiously as he sat back up on the counter so he was closer to eye level with the tall canid.

"Maybe, it was a trick of the light…"

"Very possible," the fox agreed, stifling a giggle.

Now that the wolf was standing close to the aroused fox, a thick, and distinctly male, musk filled his nose.

"I-I couldn't smell that you weren't female with the smoke and perfume and… and…"

The wolf looked back up at the fox, who was now caressing his muzzle softly.

"Listen to me wolfie, it's okay. It doesn't mean anything okay?"

"Okay…" the wolf tentatively agreed, not quite sure what was happening now, his mind still clouded with his own arousal.

"But, it did" the fox leaned down and gently took hold of the wolf's still-hard cock "feel good, didn't it?"

"Ooooof," the wolf whimpered as the soft paw began to stroke his swollen shaft.

"We're all alone here wolfie, no one has to know if I make you feel good a little longer."

The fox rubbed his fingers over the tender crown of the wolf's cockhead, making his member drip precum and getting a stifled whimper from the wolf.

The fox got up for a moment, turned around, and bent himself over the countertop again. He lifted his short skirt up, wiggling his tail as he did. He knew he had the wolf right where he wanted him, and he knew just what this needful but "straight" male wanted to hear.

"Now get over here and fuck me like the naughty vixen you thought I was." He commanded with a sly grin.

The wolf stepped forward dumbly, breathing heavy and obviously being led by the dripping member protruding from his body. As he moved closer, the fox flicked his tail up again so that it was raised invitingly. The equally needy fox gave his would-be lover a great view of his upturned rear. The tight, silky panties outlined the perfect curves of his butt. He teased the wolf by slowly lowering them just to where the bottom curve of his rump met his upper thighs, being very careful not to show off his more masculine aspects. The fox surreptitiously adjusted his erection so that it wasn't trapped against the counter-top under his body. He didn't want it squashed under him, and he could somehow tell this wolf was going to give him a really good ride.

The wolf gently caressed the smooth, red fur of the "vixen's" rump. The fur was so soft, and felt wonderful under his paw. The aroused canid let a lusty growl slip out, barely audible under his breath.

The fox shivered a little at the sound, "Yes wolfie, go on, you know you want to…fuck me now, I need it so bad."

Overcome with lust and desperate to see all of the fox's beautiful body, he pulled the fox's panties all the way down, revealing the rest of his perfectly round rear and slim thighs.

The fox's butt transfixed him. He pushed the bushy red tail up. The vulpine's bottom was all red furred except for a small amount of white fur between the cheeks that ran up onto the bottom of his tail, and also below to his white-furred balls and inner thighs. He tried to ignore the impressive length of foxcock hanging below his "vixen". He moved in close to the fox, their bodies pressed together, his throbbing wolfhood resting against the soft fur. His cock leaked pre on the fox's fur, which was very soft and felt so good against his exposed cockhead.

He didn't think twice, he'd already come too far now and the fox was right, who would know? They didn't even know each other's names. He pressed his cockhead hard against the fox's tight anus. The fox gripped the countertop as he felt himself being forced open. Luckily, the wolf was so turned on that he had produced enough precum to ease the entrance somewhat. As the fox's slickened hole gave way, the wolf pushed forward urgently, swiftly burying his wolfhood between the fox's soft, furry cheeks. As the thick length opened him up roughly and suddenly, the fox cried out.

Momentarily terrified that someone might hear, the wolf reached out and clamped his right paw around the fox's muzzle. He continued to whimper around the wolf's paw, but could not cry out now. The big wolf held him tight like that, one paw on the counter for leverage and the other firmly around his muzzle. He held still for a moment, afraid he had hurt the small fox.

After a moment, he removed his paw. He looked around nervously with the vulpine still impaled on his thick shaft.

"Um, are you okay?"

Inwardly, the fox groaned. This wolf obviously had never mounted a male before; he had a lot to learn about taking things slow. Luckily, he liked things rough occasionally and the wolf was a very nice size so he was willing to take a little initial discomfort. Given the moment's respite, he was more than ready for a good ride.

"I'm fine wolfie, now give it to me!"

The wolf grinned, his worries about mounting a male being melted away by the pure pleasure of the fox's tight rear clamping down on his hard member. He couldn't recall a female being this tight. As the fox had asked for a good ride, he began humping hard into the vulpine's tight rear. The thickness of his cock and the fox's tightness forced him to take it slow at first, but after a few minutes of huffing and puffing, the wolf's long, slow pumps had loosened up the fox enough for him to speed up a bit.

"Ohhh, yes that feels good," the fox moaned as the wolf's thick shaft opened him up wide. The fox's own member drooled precum down onto the counter. He whimpered in frustration as he was unable to paw at himself, and he knew it would break the wolf's straight fantasy if he asked him to paw him off.

Then again, this teasing felt really, really good too.

The wolf grunted as he pumped faster. He lifted up the fox's tail and watched in satisfaction as his solid meaty shaft pounded in and out of the fox's perfect rear. He loved watching his wolfhood disappear between those beautiful cheeks. He tried not to think about the fox he found so attractive being male fearing it would break his concentration.

The little tug on his tail added even more stimulation to the anal penetration and the fox gasped with the dual pleasure.

"Oh yes wolfie, pull my tail like that."

The wolf didn't hold back, he gripped the fox's bushy tail in the middle and pulled up firmly.

"Ah!" The fox gasped.

"Oh, you like that, eh." The wolf grinned and gave the fox's tail a couple more sharp tugs as he continued to pound his fat cock deep inside the willing "vixen" bent over before him.

"Oh my-ahhhh yes. Harder! Fuck me harder!!" The fox cried out.

The wolf no longer cared about keeping the fox quiet. The gasps of pleasure and the urging to take him hard made him want the fox even more. He continued to sharply yank on the fox's tail in time with his deep thrustings into his tight rear. He leaned over the fox, putting everything he had into humping the vulpine madly. Very soon he felt his knot begin to press against the needy tailhole beneath him.

The fox was in heaven now. The wolf was taking him hard and fast, and that was exactly what he wanted. This party was for mindless screwing and tonight he was a vixen in heat. He felt the wolf's huge cockhead pounding repeatedly against his pleasure spot deep inside. He just needed a little more and he knew he would cum without even touching his raging hard foxcock.

The wolf knew his knot was fully engorged and could tie with the fox now. He just wasn't sure if he should or even could with another male. His knot pressed insistently at the fox's entrance with each inward thrust.

"Um, should I—"

Before he could get the question out, his partner snarled with desperation in his voice.

"If you don't, I'll bite you. Now, tie with me!"

Whether it was out of arousal or fear for his life, it didn't matter; the wolf slammed his knot home at that moment. The sound that came from the fox wasn't quite a scream, but it wasn't far off. More like an extreme pleasure-filled yelp as his small body was overcome with the mixed pain and pleasure of his tailhole stretching hugely to allow the wolf's fist-sized knot to enter. Not to mention the wolf had yanked hard back on his tail to help ram his knot in. The fox's painfully hard cock bumped against the front of the counter he was obscenely bent over.

The wolf almost lay down on top of the willing fox as he jackhammered his trapped cock against the fox's insides. He could only take a few short moments of the tight tailhole squeezing down hard behind his sensitive knot before he howled and filled the fox with his cum. The wolf's cock slamming and spurting inside him soon triggered the fox's climax also. His eyes watered and he was nearly speechless with pleasure as his untouched foxhood pumped its load against the counter and onto the bathroom floor. The wolf filled him up with lupine cum just as his own balls were emptying in a very powerful orgasm.

Both groaned in exhaustion and felt weak. The wolf slumped against the fox, trapping him with his body as well as his cock.

"I haven't cum that hard in a long time," the wolf said with a great deal of surprise in his voice.

"Me neither...told you, you'd like it." The fox panted underneath him.

The big wolf gulped and had to admit to himself that the fox was right. It was the best sex he'd had in a really long time.

After a few minutes of panting for breath and enjoying the afterglow, the wolf's knot had finally shrunk enough for him to pull out of the well-satisfied fox.

He looked a bit guilty as he cleaned himself off and began to get dressed. He sighed as he caught the fox looking curiously at him.

"Now, what do I do?"

"Well, if you ever think you're ready to try some more, just give me a call."

The fox picked up his panties and retrieved a pen that had

fallen from the pocket of the wolf's discarded jeans. He scribbled something onto the crotch of the panties and tossed them to the wolf, who caught them deftly. The wolf just watched, wondering if he should say something, as the fox then cleaned off his shrinking cock before it shrunk back into his sheath. The fox smiled sweetly at the wolf as he unlocked the bathroom door.

"Thanks for a really nice time, wolfie." He said as he opened the door. "You're a natural," he added as he left, "sexy."

"But?" He looked up just in time to see the fox's bushy tail disappearing as the door closed behind him.

The wolf scratched his head and wondered what to do next as he looked down at the silky, white panties.

"Trevor 555-9433"

AFTER THE TRICK

Trevor blinked as he stepped back out into the world of noisy music and swirling lights from the quiet sanctum of the bathroom. He smoothed down his skirt and wandered around the corner towards the dancehall. He smiled as he saw a familiar sight. A large, grey wolf approached him. He walked arm in arm with a twink of a bunny, whom the fox also knew well.

"Hello foxy," the big wolf grinned at him.

Trevor beamed and blushed a little. He always felt that submissive rush even when Sinclair simply greeted him.

"Heyyy," Jamie the bunny said hello in the gayest way possible.

Trevor and Jamie looked each other up and down with a grin, they'd worn nearly the same outfit. While Trevor had gone with "Catholic schoolgirl" for this costume party, Jamie had opted for "naughty cheerleader". The rabbit's ripped fishnet stockings, dark pleated skirt and tight leather top contrasted greatly with Trevor's white knee-high socks, checked skirt, white shirt and matching sweater. Sinclair was dressed rather more masculinely in full regalia as a Scottish highlander complete with kilt and sporran.

Sinclair looked between the two and got an idea. "Oh, this is too good to pass up." He swung his other arm around Trevor's waist and pulled the fox close to him. "You're coming with us foxy."

Trevor blushed hotly, he was getting turned on again and he could feel the coolness of the air slipping under his skirt and across his plump sheath. "Ooh, yes sir," he grinned.

The wolf slipped his paws lower to give his "girls" a gentle squeeze as they walked toward the door. His paw went under Jamie's skirt and caressed the smooth black of the satin panties the bunny was wearing. He gave Jamie's panty-covered bottom a squeeze, making the rabbit jump slightly. He wondered what Trevor was wearing underneath and moved to find out. When his paw found Trevor's perfect little rump, his paw encountered only bare fur. His cock immediately throbbed in his sheath and he turned to face the fox with mock seriousness.

"You naughty girl," he said while licking his lips. "You went out in public bare-bottomed?"

Trevor blushed hard to the tips of ears and he tried to explain about the wolf and the bathroom. Sinclair slipped a finger under the vulpine's tail and teased his moist, recently used tailhole. He cut Trevor off mid-explanation.

"Doesn't matter fox, you're going over my knee as soon as we get home."

Trevor could now feel his cock throbbing under his skirt and he tried to mentally keep it from tenting his skirt as the three furs stepped outside the club and made their way to Sinclair's car. Jamie smirked at Trevor when the wolf's back was to them to open the car's doors.

"Ladies," he said as he opened the rear door and gestured inside. Trevor got in first, inadvertently giving Jamie a clear view of his bare bottom as he leaned into the car. "Why don't you two get started," he whispered in one of the rabbit's long ears.

With a grin, Jamie hopped into the back seat after Trevor.

Sinclair closed the door behind them and walked around to

the driver's side. Once he'd started the engine, his eyes flickered to the rear view mirror. Jamie was already tenderly nipping Trevor's neck with his long, lapine teeth. The bunny had one paw under Trevor's skirt and was clearly stroking the fox. Sinclair figured he'd better hurry home before Trevor made a mess in his car.

Sinclair's black car screeched out of its parking space and roared as the wolf gunned the engine.

In the back seat, Trevor tried to resist Jamie's flirtations. He didn't want to get into more trouble than he was already in and obviously didn't know that Sinclair had told Jamie to get a jump on things, so to speak.

The fox whimpered as Jamie's soft-furred, expert paw moved up and down the length of his shaft. The fox's cock was now fully extended from his sheath and he wouldn't be able to hide his arousal under his short skirt if he tried.

Jamie pulled away from nibbling at his neck for a moment and looked at him.

"Huh, that's weird."

"Wh-what?" Trevor stammered, not the thing you want to

hear when someone is handling your cock.

"Your eyes, they're green again."

Trevor blinked, a little confused.

"They looked blue in the club, must've been the light."

"Oh," Trevor replied, not really thinking clearly right now as Jamie squeezed slowly up the length of his shaft from base to tip.

The bunny licked his lips with hunger. Trevor was nicely hung, especially for a little fox his size. The bunny's little puff of a tail twitched and he hoped Sinclair would either let or make the fox mount him by the end of the night. His paw was idly stroking Trevor's slick precum across his cocktip as he thought about being filled. He was so preoccupied that he didn't notice the car had stopped.

"We-we're here," Trevor moaned, trying not to cum again. He'd cum earlier while being mounted in the bathroom, but he'd climaxed without touching himself. This was the first time tonight someone had had their paws on his foxhood and it wasn't taking much to get him really close to the edge again. It didn't help that Jamie knew exactly where to touch him.

The cool night air broke the moment when Sinclair opened Trevor's door. For the fox, it was just in time as he had been feeling the pressure of an impending orgasm building up again.

Sinclair reached out his paw for Trevor's to help him up. The wolf's large paw completely covered the fox's smaller, feminine paw. Sinclair smiled as his girly fox stepped out of the car. He looked back at Jamie, who was eagerly licking vulpine precum from his fingertips. Trevor moved to his left and Sinclair extended a paw to the bunny.

"Right this way, ladies," Sinclair remarked as he led them to the door. He was in wolf Heaven. He could feel his wolfhood growing thick and hard already as he walked with a submissive girly boi on both arms.

148

Once inside, Jamie and Trevor scurried away to the bedroom. Sinclair followed at his own pace, suppressing a chuckle at how eager those two were. He began to strip off his costume as he approached his bedroom door. He could already hear Trevor's familiar moans of pleasure and he wondered just what that bunny was doing to him.

Sinclair had only his kilt left to remove when he walked into the bedroom. It hit the ground with a heavy thump as he slipped it off.

Jamie's head was bobbing up and down under Trevor's skirt as the fox tried to speak.

"You're bare under there too," he managed to get out after a second as he took in the wonderful sight of Sinclair's fully hard and ready wolfcock.

The wolf chuckled, "Real highlanders always are," he replied.

Sinclair pulled Jamie away. He could hear the suction noise as Trevor's thick cock left the rabbit's mouth. He pulled Trevor up gently and sat down on the bed where the fox had been lying.

"Besides," he said as he began to pull Trevor over his knee, a position the fox knew well, "your skirt is a lot shorter."

Trevor whimpered and felt a familiar flush of fear, anticipation and need as he was pulled over the wolf's powerful, naked thighs. He groaned when he felt Sinclair's erection pressing against him through the short skirt, hoping he'd get to feel that later. He gripped Sinclair's bare knee, knowing what was to come. He felt coolness across his bare bottom as the wolf lifted up his skirt. Jamie stood aside and watched eagerly as the wolf began to slowly caress the fox's exposed rear. The rabbit felt himself throb in his panties as the wolf's paw moved down to gently cup and stroke Trevor's balls. Trevor moaned and Jamie whimpered with need.

Trevor shut his eyes and bit his lip as the first swat came.

Sinclair wasted no time in working his bottom hard and fast. The fox whimpered and bit his finger to stifle a squeak as the wolf's large paw nearly covered his entire rump with each swat. Sinclair moved quickly from left to right, making sure each cheek got equal attention.

Jamie moved a paw under his skirt and began to stroke himself through his panties. The smoothness of the black satin felt amazing against his fully hard cock as his fingers teased along the edges of his cocktip. Sinclair noticed what he was doing out of the corner of his eye.

"Bunny, make yourself useful and go get my brush," he ordered the rabbit.

"Yes, sir," Jamie replied, reluctantly stopping playing with himself to go into the nightstand where Sinclair kept the heavy, wooden hairbrush he kept for just such an occasion.

"Not the brush, sir please," Trevor begged.

The fox's pleas made Sinclair's cock bulge with arousal. He was always amazed at how well Trevor knew how to get to him.

"Hurry up," he snapped at Jamie.

"I can't find it," Jamie replied with desperation as he rifled through the wolf's toy drawer.

Sinclair gently teased under Trevor's tail while he waited. The fox moaned as Sinclair fingered his little hole that had already been used once tonight.

"Bunny if you don't put that brush in my paw in five seconds, I'll make you sit and watch us all night."

The rabbit's heart pounded in his chest as he searched in desperation. Watching Sinclair use and abuse the fox all night without being able to participate would be torture. Luckily, he found the wolf's favourite brush and dashed back to the bed to give it to him.

Sinclair smiled as he felt the smooth wooden handle being

placed urgently into his paw. He gently stroked Trevor's head-fur with the bristled side and teased the rough bristles along the edges of the fox's sensitive ears.

"Now you're really gonna get it foxy," he said with a growl.

Trevor whimpered. "Please sir, I'll be a good girl," he gasped as he felt Sinclair softly brushing the fur of his vulnerable bottom. Between his legs, his foxhood dripped precum onto the floor.

Sinclair continued to tease Trevor as he loved the whimpering and begging his little vixen did so well. "Jamie, take off your skirt," he ordered the other submissive, as he began to slowly and firmly swat Trevor's rear with the thick, wooden brush.

Jamie complied wordlessly. He quickly slipped the skirt off and tossed it on the floor near where Sinclair's kilt had landed.

"Now, come over here where I can see you."

Jamie stepped in front of Sinclair. The wolf looked the rabbit up and down slowly while still spanking Trevor a little harder and a little faster with the brush.

Jamie was tall for a rabbit. The wolf liked the way the black stockings contrasted with Jamie's gray fur and made his slim legs look even longer. The stockings were high and stopped at Jamie's thighs, leaving a small amount of grey fur exposed between the tops of the stockings and the smooth black panties the rabbit wore. The panties were bulging out at the front and the length of Jamie's cock could be clearly seen, the constant sound of the brush on Trevor's bare bottom and the fox's moans and gasps of pleasure and pain kept him hard and throbbing. A bit of Jamie's flat stomach was exposed and the wolf could see the slight dip in his fur where his navel was.

"On your knees."

Jamie sunk to his knees in front of Sinclair immediately. His eyes locked with Sinclair's as he tried to ignore the kicking, wriggling fox over the wolf's knee.

The heavy spanking continued as Sinclair dominated Jamie from the bed.

"Now, touch yourself. You know how."

Jamie knew exactly what Sinclair meant and he began to stroke the long lump of his cock through his smooth panties. Sinclair wanted him to keep up the feminine act as long as possible and not pull out his cock and stroke himself as he normally would. They'd played this game before so Jamie teased himself the way a doe would. His fingertips caressed along the crown of his cockhead while still held tightly inside the black panties. Jamie moaned and bucked his hips slightly, his tail twitched and he was acutely aware of how empty his tailhole felt. He needed to be filled badly tonight.

Sinclair returned his attention to his other little pet, whom he had never stopped spanking. Tears ran from the fox's eyes and along his muzzle as the long, hard punishment continued. The wolf slowed down a little to savour Trevor's reactions.

He gave the fox's right cheek a hard smack. Trevor cringed and wriggled on his knee. He hit the left side just as hard and the fox shook in pain, but reacted by raising his bottom into the air, signaling that he wanted it. The next smack was in the middle, where Trevor's cheeks met his thighs and the fox moaned as his tender spot was swatted and the impact sent a jolt of pleasure to his cock and another small splatter of precum hit the floor.

Sinclair continued to toy with Trevor in this way. The swats from the brush were very hard, but were slower in coming. Sinclair used his paw that had been supporting Trevor's chest to find and squeeze one of the fox's nipples. Trevor squeaked a little at this new pain.

"Good boy," Sinclair growled.

Sinclair decided to finish up with a quick rain of extremely hard smacks to Trevor's bottom and upper thighs. The little fox wriggled around in Sinclair's firm grasp. The wolf enjoyed watching the small, feminine male's legs kicking in the air as he was spanked soundly. He smiled at how cute Trevor's legs looked in their knee-high white socks and little black shoes.

"S-sir?" Jamie squeaked from his position, his voice shaky.

Sinclair looked up to see Jamie's panties were now slick with precum and the rabbit's firm thighs were beginning to buck wildly as he teased his cocktip through his panties. He knew Jamie was trying to get his attention because he was likely seconds away from climaxing, but didn't want to do so without permission. Staying true to allowing the wolf control over him meant more than the pleasure he desperately wanted now that he was so close to the edge.

"Better slow down there, Bunny," Sinclair responded.

"Yes, sir," the rabbit moaned.

Jamie's paw slowed down and he tried to avoid stimulating his cockhead. He instead stroked along his shaft and occasionally moved lower between his legs to squeeze his balls gently in their smooth, satin pocket.

Trevor was crying, his bare bottom burned with the hard, fast spanking, but his cock throbbed with need and he humped his hips upwards to meet the brush as it rained down on his tender cheeks. He gently nibbled on the wolf's knee. He felt like every nerve in his body was on edge as he bucked and wriggled on Sinclair's strong thighs. His eyes shot open when the stimulation to his backside suddenly stopped and Sinclair was lifting him up. The wolf quickly stripped the skirt off of him. Trevor gasped and quickly lifted his tail out of the way as the strong wolf lowered him down. He felt Sinclair's thick cock sliding up between his abused cheeks for a moment before the wolf found his hole expertly.

Trevor cried out as Sinclair pulled him down into his lap

and the thick cock opened him up wide. Of course, Sinclair was much bigger than the wolf who had taken him at the club so even though the fox had already been used once tonight it still hurt as he was spread out wider than before. He moaned as he felt the wolfcock pressing hard against his prostate. Precum flowed down the length of his thick shaft as he settled into Sinclair's embrace. He opened his eyes and saw himself in the mirror across from Sinclair's bed.

Jamie was finding it hard to not cum from watching the scene. Trevor looked incredibly hot. The fox was still fully clothed on top. On the bottom he still wore the cute little black shoes and long socks of his schoolgirl outfit, but he was bare from the tops of his socks to the bottom of his shirt. His tail was pinned against his back and when his legs parted slightly, Jamie could see Sinclair's full balls dangling beneath them. The fox moaned and closed his slim thighs and squeezed his rump down on the thick invader under his tail. This made him feel even tighter to the powerful wolf who held him.

Sinclair looked past Trevor's shoulder, which he had been biting down on, to see Jamie.

"Bunny, why don't you help out our little vixen."

Jamie licked his lips and crawled on his paws and knees over to the edge of the bed. He sat up on his knees and began to slowly lick Trevor's foxhood up and down. He collected the dripping precum from along Trevor's shaft and licked all around the fur of his sheath where some precum had collected.

The fox moaned as Jamie lapped at his cock and fondled his full balls with his soft paws. He nearly came when the rabbit squeezed his balls gently and his body shivered with pleasure once Jamie's tongue was on his cocktip, lapping up the freely flowing precum.

"We've got to teach our naughty vixen a lesson, don't we?"

Sinclair asked rhetorically as he nibbled along Trevor's neck and ears.

The variety of sensations was overwhelming and Trevor knew he couldn't last much longer. His bottom still burned from the hard spanking and he could feel every tender nerve as his rump rubbed against the rough fur of Sinclair's groin. Sinclair occasionally tugged his tail up out of the way and that stimulated the feeling around his full tailhole as the wolf ground his thick knot against his tiny opening. His slim thighs quivered as Jamie eagerly lapped at his drooling cockhead and fondled his full balls. Trevor had just about gotten hold of himself when Sinclair moved his paws to his hips and began to jackhammer him up and down in his lap. Trevor moaned like a vixen as the thick cock thrust up and down inside him.

Sensing that he was close, Jamie took the fox's thick length as deep into his mouth as he could manage. His tongue continued to lick at the underside of the foxcock while he sucked hard.

Trevor's whole body tensed up and he felt his balls pulse with need. He cried out as he came hard for the second time that night. Cum rushed up his shaft and filled the rabbit's waiting mouth. Jamie swallowed everything Trevor fed him. The fox's backside clamped down on the huge wolfcock inside him as he climaxed. He leaned his neck to the side as the pleasure flowed over him and Sinclair took immediate advantage and clamped his lupine jaws around his exposed neck. Trevor whimpered like a trapped animal, held tightly between the wolf's cock and teeth and the rabbit's sucking muzzle.

Once he had sucked Trevor dry, Jamie slowly withdrew and sat back on his knees. His long cock was still clearly outlined in his panties. Sinclair also released the exhausted fox by lifting him up off of his rock hard wolfhood. He gently laid Trevor down on the bed while tenderly licking his cheeks and muzzle.

"Rest a moment foxy, I'm going to need you in a minute."

Trevor was puzzled, but didn't argue. He lay his head down and closed his eyes, taking the time given to enjoy the powerful afterglow and regain his energy.

"Now then," Sinclair stood up and stretched before holding out his paw to Jamie, "to deal with you."

Jamie took the offered paw and let Sinclair pull him to his feet. The rabbit's eyes followed the wolf's thick cock. He knew Sinclair hadn't cum in Trevor so he was eagerly hoping he'd be the one to be filled with the wolf's seed tonight. His heart pounded at the thought. He gasped as he felt the wolf's paw between his legs, cupping his balls.

"Hmm, very nice outfit there bunny," Sinclair growled as he turned the rabbit around. "Nice and tight, those panties really show off your butt quite nicely."

"Thank you, sir," Jamie moaned as Sinclair manipulated his balls and admired his panty-clad bottom. He closed his eyes and sighed happily as he felt the wolf's other paw smacking soundly against his tiny bottom. "Yessss," he moaned.

Sinclair grinned as Jamie leaned over, purely running on instinct. Trevor sat up as he felt Jamie lean against the mattress. He looked up to see what was happening now. Even though he'd cum twice tonight, the sight of the masculine, naked wolf fondling and spanking the slim, feminine bunny who was bending over willingly was too hot not to cause Trevor's exhausted foxhood to stir and come to life again.

The fact that Jamie was still dressed except for his discarded skirt made the scene even hotter. The rabbit's cock still tented the front of his panties badly, but Jamie wasn't touching himself anymore. He was leaning both paws on the edge of the bed and pushing his rump up towards Sinclair's quickly swatting paw.

For his part, Sinclair really enjoyed spanking the little bunny in his panties. The cool satin felt good against his palm and made a satisfying smacking sound. He watched the bunny's little cotton tail twitching with each firm swat to his petite bottom.

Out of the corner of his eye, Trevor noticed one of Sinclair's other favourite toys on top of the pile in the open toy drawer. He decided to be helpful and picked it up.

"Oh, thank you Trevor," Sinclair smiled at the playful fox as he offered him the leather strap.

Jamie kept his eyes closed tightly as he focused on the sensations the wolf was inflicting on his body. He gasped loudly as the sensation suddenly changed. He moaned and bent over even more as Sinclair used the strap on his bottom, hard and fast. It made a loud smack against his smooth panties and the rabbit could feel the stinging through to his bones and he loved it.

Sinclair moved his paw from the rabbit's balls to hold him by the shoulder instead, but Trevor had decided to return the other's favour and Jamie soon felt the fox's smaller paws rubbing his balls and hard shaft through the front of his panties. Jamie still had his eyes closed and moaned as he rode the waves of pain and pleasure that his companions were pulling from his body.

The wolf worked Jamie's bottom hard and fast with the leather strap. He looked over to his fox and saw that Trevor was once again rock hard. 'Perfect,' he thought.

"Trevor, lie on your back in the middle of the bed."

"Okay," Trevor bounced over to the center of the bed as ordered. He looked down and saw that his foxhood was standing up, full and hard, from his sheath.

Sinclair pushed his hand down the back of Jamie's panties and slowly teased underneath his little white tail.

"Bunny wants to get filled tonight, doesn't he?"

"Ooh, yes sir," Jamie moaned and pushed back against the wolf's probing finger.

"Good, because you're going to get it from both of us tonight."

Jamie went weak at the knees and nearly fell over at those words. Unlike some people, he hadn't gotten off at the club and had been close to it repeatedly tonight. He was desperate now and the thought of both of those thick cocks in him one after the other was just what he needed. He gasped when Sinclair yanked his panties off and his hard cock was finally released. He opened his eyes to see Trevor's waiting cock. Sinclair gave his naked behind a final hard smack with the strap and commanded him to get on the foxcock now.

Jamie hopped up onto the bed on all fours. His panties dangled from one foot for a moment before falling to the floor, which was gradually becoming littered with their clothes. He crawled over to Trevor and straddled the fox's thighs. Jamie leaned down and took Trevor's cock into his muzzle and began to suck and lick, letting plenty of spit build up and flow down the vulpine's thick shaft.

Trevor gasped and moaned as the rabbit teased his sensitive foxhood. He helped guide Jamie down as the rabbit crouched over him once his cock was nice and wet.

Jamie slowly placed Trevor's slick cockhead against his tight bunnyhole and began to push the fox in. He squeaked as Trevor's thick cockhead opened him up. He shuddered through the initial pain and sighed happily as he got past the crown of Trevor's cockhead and allowed the thick shaft to slide into his stretched hole.

As Jamie's insides adjusted to the first cock he'd taken tonight, Sinclair had noticed Trevor sweating profusely and decided to help. He pulled the little fox's warm sweater off and removed his shoes, leaving Trevor wearing only his white shirt and his long, white schoolgirl socks.

Sinclair stood aside to watch as Jamie began to slowly ride

the fox's cock. He admired the way Trevor's foxhood sunk into Jamie's tight bottom each time the bunny rode up and down. He licked his lips with anticipation as he watched the fox's thick cock sliding deep into that tight rabbit hole.

Trevor took hold of Jamie's cock, which was gently bouncing up and down as the bunny rode him. His soft foxy paws slowly rubbed up and down the rabbit's tender, needy shaft making Jamie moan and hump himself on Trevor's cock a little harder. Trevor also thrust upwards to meet Jamie's humping bottom, making his thick foxhood slam hard into Jamie's insides.

That was when the pair felt the weight of the bed shift and Trevor looked back to see Sinclair crawling up toward them on all fours. The fox could also see the wolf's long, thick cock dripping and hanging between his legs. Trevor assumed Sinclair would make him suck him off while he Jamie rode his cock, but he was wrong.

The wolf crept up behind Jamie and pushed his long, lupine muzzle under his full bottom and began to lick softly. The pair of submissive furs moaned as they both felt the wolf's long tongue going to work. Jamie felt it softly caressing his stretched hole as Trevor's cock slammed into him and Trevor felt it sliding up and down the sensitive underside of his shaft as he took the bunny hard.

Sinclair then sat up and held Jamie's hips down so that he was still. The pair were confused, but didn't say anything. They let their wolf lead the way even though they were both on the brink of cumming together. Sinclair pushed Jamie forward a little bit. The rabbit leaned over obligingly. He was in bliss. He was filled with a thick cock and his own cock was being teased by the fox's soft fur while the dominant wolf man-handled him. He relaxed until he felt something unexpected.

Sinclair pressed his thick cocktip against Jamie's full tailhole and began to press forward. Jamie shuddered and cried out as his tight bunny bottom began to stretch open even more.

"I told you you'd get it from both of us tonight," Sinclair explained with a growl as he continued to push hard against the bunny's full bottom.

Naturally, Jamie had intended to be taken by them one at a time. He panicked for a moment as he'd never taken so much at once before, but his cock ignored his mind's worries and sent a shot of precum all the way to Trevor's muzzle where it landed along the side of the fox's nose. Jamie spread his hips slightly and leaned closer to Trevor, who held his head gently against his chest in a comforting way as he knew this was difficult. He also knew that it was really hot and was a little jealous that it wasn't him being pinned and double-penetrated by the two of them.

Jamie's paws clenched the bed as Sinclair's cockhead entered him fully with a pop. The rest of the wolf's shaft slid in easier once the head was inside. Sinclair gritted his teeth and moaned as he pressed forward. He could feel his cock sliding against Trevor's thick shaft. Trevor whimpered in response as he felt the wolfhood sliding up along his shaft. Soon, Sinclair's hips rested against the rabbit's small, full bottom. The three of them held still for a moment, mostly allowing Jamie to adjust to the extreme amount of stretching his insides were undergoing.

Soon the pain slowly faded and Jamie was left feeling full, more full than he'd ever felt before. It hurt, but it felt right and once Sinclair began to move him back and forth, the two cocks inside him felt absolutely wonderful as they pressed against every nerve and tender spot inside him at once. There was so much pressure on his prostate at this point that he began cumming immediately, giving his balls a much needed release and still leaving his cock rock hard as Sinclair leaned back and Jamie began to rock back and forth, up and down, of his own accord.

160

Trevor and Sinclair held still and enjoyed the feeling of the incredible tightness around them and the feeling of their cocks sliding against each other and let Jamie control the three-way mating.

Sinclair and Jamie had been on edge for so long that they both felt themselves getting close to climaxing quickly. Jamie bore down and increased his speed, desperate to feel the wolf and fox filling him with their seed. He panted and moaned, pushing himself to go faster, whimpering as his body stretched out and all he felt was the intense pleasure of the two thick cocks pumping into him.

Sinclair felt himself getting closer and closer. He reached down and squeezed himself behind his fully-formed knot. He ground his knot against the outside of Jamie's full tailhole and howled as his balls pulled close to his body and he released a massive load of wolf cum into the bunny's depths.

The sudden slickness of Sinclair's load rushing over his cock, made Trevor squeal and hump upwards hard. Jamie cried out as the thick foxcock hilted even deeper inside him. Sinclair held himself inside Jamie, wanting to keep them together as one until both the others had finished. Trevor couldn't hold on any longer due to the added slickness and Jamie squeezing down on him. The fox came too, for the third time that night. He gasped as his balls were drained yet again.

Jamie was on the edge now too. His partners helped him through with whispers of encouragement. Sinclair leaned close and whispered in his ears while pushing his wolfhood as deep as he could. Trevor pushed up and held himself deep as well. He also continued to tease the rabbit's long cock by rubbing his soft-furred paws back and forth over it while the underside was lying in Trevor's soft bellyfur.

"Cum for us bunny."

"You know you want to."

"You need to."

"Cum while we're both inside you."

"Little bunny wants to cum so bad."

"Do it now Jamie, spurt all over me."

Jamie cried out and his body squeezed down hard on the two cocks inside him as he came harder than he'd ever cum before. His shot his seed all over Trevor's chest. The fox kept pumping his paws up and down on his spurting cock, draining his balls fully. Sinclair licked and nibbled his neck as Jamie rode out his incredible climax.

Once he had ridden his orgasm to the end, Jamie sat and trembled, overwhelmed by the experience.

"S-sir, can you?"

Sinclair leaned up and gently nipped Jamie's ear before slowly pulling his wolfhood out of the bunny's much-abused bottom. Jamie squeezed closed around Trevor's cock as a flood of cum began to seep through his stretched tailhole. The bunny lifted himself slowly off of Trevor's foxhood and rolled over to his side.

The big wolf lay down on the bed between his two submissive partners and wrapped an arm around each of them. The fox and the bunny snuggled close to the wolf and he nuzzled each of them affectionately. The three lay there, panting and exhausted, for a long while as they came down from the incredible natural high they'd gone through.

"That was incredible…" Jamie mumbled sleepily.

Sinclair sighed contently.

Trevor bit his lip a little nervously, "I wanna go next…" he said shyly.

The wolf smiled and hugged them both close to him.

"Works for me."

FuzzWolf

Author's Notes

Sexual Predator

While not the first story I wrote with these characters, this is the first time that Trevor and Sinclair meet.

Something I Can Never Have

All the characters in these tales reflect different aspects of my own personality. Lewis is me when I was in my early twenties and a bit emo. Ironically, finding the fandom is what cheered me up.

Some Like it Rough

Parts of this story are based on a real life experience, I'll let the readers try and guess which parts. This story was very nearly lost to a hard drive crash, but luckily I had e-mailed an early draft to Teiran so I was able to continue it from where I'd left off.

Stud Exercise Program

This was originally written off the cuff for a mailing list that sadly, no longer exists. I wrote and posted this from my webTV! I've edited it twice since to bring it more up to date with my writing style, but forgive me if it's still a little clunky in places. This is one of my earliest stories.

Advanced Stretching

It only took four years, but I continued *Stud Exercise Program*. I know it kinda ends on a cliffhanger, but you can use your imagination as to what happens next.

Naughty Boy's Lesson

This one was actually written prior to Sexual Predator and is an early attempt at first-person narration. I know it can be a bit odd to read a role-play scenario like this when so much of the role-playing is mental so think of this story as Trevor writing the experience down in his diary.

Pulled Over

I hope everyone enjoyed the twist at the end of this one. This one was just a fun random romp for Trevor and introduced Catch, whom I plan to write about again.

A Trick of the Light

This was first published in early 2003 in FurNation Magazine #3. It was later reprinted in the first FurNation Compendium. I'm also happy to report it has been included on Yiffstar.com's list of recommended Male/Male stories.

After the Trick

This is a brand new story, completed in March of 2007 on a day I called in sick to work. You shouldn't really care about that, I just find it amusing. :-)

If you've enjoyed these tales of Trevor and his friends, you can find more foxy adventures and a lot more at my website: www.FuzzWolf.com

Please feel free to write to me with any comments on my stories at FuzzWolf@FurPlanet.com

About the Author

FuzzWolf has been active in the furry fandom for nearly ten years. He began writing on mailing lists in 1999 and later decided to try his hand at stories rather than just RP sessions.

FuzzWolf is currently working part-time at FurNation as the editor of the FurNation Anthology magazine and as a talent scout and comic layout person. He also works a full-time job and still manages to squeeze in time for setting up and attending meets for the local furry community.

He lives with his mate, Teiran, in Texas.

www.ingramcontent.com/pod-product-compliance
Lightning Source LLC
Chambersburg PA
CBHW051836020726
47502CB00005B/1813

* 9 7 8 1 9 3 5 5 9 9 0 0 5 *